Surrendered Heart

STEPHANIE PERRY MOORE

The Negro National Anthem

Lift every voice and sing
Till earth and heaven ring,
Ring with the harmonies of Liberty;
Let our rejoicing rise
High as the listening skies,
Let it resound loud as the rolling sea.
Sing a song, full of the faith that the dark past has taught us,
Sing a song, full of the hope that the present has brought us,
Facing the rising sun, of our new day begun
Let us march on till victory is won.

So begins the Black National Anthem, by James Weldon Johnson in 1900. Lift Every Voice is the name of the joint imprint of The Institute for Black Family Development and Moody Publishers, a division of the Moody Bible Institute.

Our vision is to advance the cause of Christ through publishing African-American Christians who educate, edify, and disciple Christians in the church community through quality books written for African-Americans.

The Institute for Black Family Development is a national Christian organization. It offers degreed and non-degreed training nationally and internationally to established and emerging leaders from churches and Christian organizations. To learn more about The Institute for Black Family Development, write us at:

The Institute for Black Family Development
15151 Faust
Detroit, MI 48223

Since 1984, Moody Publishers has been dedicated to equip and motivate people to advance the cause of Christ by publishing evangelical Christian literature and other media for all ages, around the world. Because we are a ministry of the Moody Bible Institute of Chicago, a portion of the proceeds from the sale of this book go to train the next generation of Christian leaders.

Moody Publishers
c/o Moody Publishers Ministries
820 N. LaSalle Blvd.
Chicago, IL 60610

Surrendered Heart

STEPHANIE PERRY MOORE

ISBN: 0-8024-4240-4

5 7 9 10 8 6
Printed in the United States of America

For my paternal grandparents,
Rev. Dewey E. Perry, Sr.
and
Mrs. Lizzie Mae Dennis Perry.
You two have taught me what
is important in this life . . .
to love family and tell the world
about Jesus Christ.
Thanks for praying for my writing.
It touched
my heart and
God heard you!

Contents

Acknowledgments

As I reflect on the tragedy that happened September 11, 2001, my heart aches. The thought of how so many died is not settling to my soul. However, to give myself peace of mind, I just pray that in those final moments, those that did not know the Lord accepted Christ. And what about those of us who are still here? This book is special to me because the main issue of the novel is salvation. Thanks to all who help me spread God's message.

To my parents, Franklin and Shirley Perry: I have a THANKFUL HEART because you raised me in a godly home. I am a better person because I've always known the Lord. So glad you two are my mom and dad!

To my publishing company, Moody Press, especially George Peterson (selling all those books): I have a GRATEFUL HEART because you all believed in me enough to publish the Payton Skky series. I have touched the lives of many because you have gotten my works out there. So thrilled to be a part of Lift Every Voice!

To my reading pool, Annie Brown, Sierra Hunter, Drea Johnson, Cole Smith, and Trace Williams and my assistant, Nakia Austin: I have a KIND HEART because of your wonderful examples of friendship and sacrifice. I truly appreciated your taking the time to make this novel the best it could be. So blessed that I could count on you!

To my boss, Mel Banks II, and the rest of the Nia Pulishing Family, Michele, Kim, Ulysses, Darryl, Shelley, Daya, Kim, Thomas, and Keith: I possess a HAPPY HEART because I love working for a company whose main objective is telling people about Jesus. I'm glad we are able to weather storms and continue stronger as a unit. So fortunate I've found a job that can use my editorial talents!

To my daughters, Sydni and Sheldyn: I have a LOVABLE HEART because of how I feel for you two. I'm proud of how well you both are doing in school! So in awe . . . that I am your mom!

To my husband, Derrick Moore: I have a SECURE HEART because I know that we are one 'til death do us part. I pray for your strength and headship. So full with how much you love me!

To the reader, wherever you are: I know I have a CARING HEART because of how badly I want you to be saved. I hope this novel blesses your life. So grateful you gave this book a try!

And to my Lord, Jesus Chirst: I have a SURRENDERED HEART. I fully give my life to you. Thanks for the vision, craft, and outlet to do what I do. I pray this book brings people into a right relationship with you, so that whenever the end of their life comes, it won't be the end!

1

Embracing the Good

My feet were planted firmly on the ground, but it felt as if I were a part of the beautiful sky. I was closer to God than I had been my whole life. My head was more clear and my heart was more His. The unsure feeling of who I was subsided.

"Lord, thank You," I cried. "I'm so grateful that You stuck by me. You are the truth, the way, and the light. The only thing that is important is pleasing You. I have given all of my trouble to You, and now I am free. I'm a new Payton Skky. I want to walk a life that pleases You."

I completely loved the Lamb of God. I was happy to give my problems to God. With His help I could live a victorious Christian life.

As soon as I made it to my cold bedroom the phone rang.

"Hello?"

"Hey," Tad said in a way that melted my heart.

"Oh, hey. You made it home."

"Yeah, I just wanted to let you know that I got here safely. I really enjoyed our evening," he told me.

He was such a gentleman. We had come from my father's Christmas party at the car dealership. Tad Taylor, my former boyfriend, meant more to me than I wanted to admit. Since I had taken him through so much, Tad decided we didn't need to be together.

That night we didn't kiss, hold hands, or do anything romantic, but it felt so right just being with him. Though he was dating another girl, I was starting to realize that, deep within, I was hoping we could be more than friends again. If we ever were, I knew I would not let go of such a special guy.

"I really enjoyed our time together, too," I told him.

We spent another ten minutes on the phone talking about our Christmas plans. He was leaving the next day to go with the University of Georgia football team to the bowl game in Florida. I was going to spend the first part of Christmas Day with my family and then go to Conyers to spend time at my grandparents' house.

"Do you think you'll be able to go to the bowl game?" Tad asked me sweetly.

"I don't know. Going down to Florida sounds mighty appealing, but I don't know if I can."

"Well, I have some extra tickets, so if you want to go just let me know."

"Thanks for asking. Merry Christmas, Tad. I hope you get a chance to play in the game and show off."

"I don't know about all of that, but I hope we win."

"You're always so modest, Tad," I told him.

"I don't look at it that way. I'd say I'm just humble. This talent comes from the Lord."

"Yeah, what are you thinking about? You're kind of quiet," I said after an unusual silence.

"I was just thinking about when I first met you. Payton, you blew me away with your beauty. Looking at you made me feel special."

Inside I was breaking. As sweet as he was, I had messed up. I treated him ten times worse than anyone deserved, especially him.

His phone clicked for another call, which was a good thing because I didn't know how to respond to his compliment. No matter how fond he was of me, I wasn't his girl anymore. When he came back to the phone and told me it was Vonda, a girl from his hometown, whom he was dating. I knew that he was moving on without me.

"Rain, what's wrong?" I asked in a panic as my best friend from high school entered my room with bloodshot eyes.

She stretched out her arms as if she wanted me to hug her. As we embraced, the tears started flowing from her eyes. She cried as if her whole world had fallen apart.

"Rain, talk to me. What's wrong?"

I wondered what could have her so upset. *Did she have a car accident? Is someone in her family hurt? Or worse, did someone die?* While terrible thoughts raced through my mind, she continued to cry uncontrollably.

She still wouldn't speak so I prayed to myself. *Lord, how am I supposed to help her when she won't talk to me? My friend is in my arms breaking down. Help me get it together to open her up. If she won't, then please don't let the situation get any worse.*

Finally she said, "It's Tyson."

Tyson was her boyfriend all during high school and he was sweet. He didn't go to Lucy Laney with us; he went to

12

school across town. Rain and Tyson were inseparable. They even went to college in the same city to be near each other. Rain went to Spelman while Tyson went to Georgia Tech.

"Do you want to talk about it?" I asked, handing her a tissue.

"It was just like what happened last year in high school with Dakari." Rain spoke in a soft, sad tone. "A couple of girls keep coming on to him at Georgia Tech. He wants me to make a choice whether I want to be with him physically or not. I want to be with him, but I want to wait until we're married. I thought he would understand. I got my Bible so that we could pray through it. Girl, he took my Bible and threw it across the room! He was so mad. He said he was faithful to me and when he wanted to take the relationship further he thought I would. He said I was wasting his time. He told me that by keeping the good-girl act I wasn't going to get anybody. He used to tell me that he loved the fact that I was a virgin."

I explained, "Maybe he was just saying what he knew you wanted to hear. I know it hurts back then because I've been there. I'm so happy that you and Dakari didn't get intimately involved. Imagine how much worse you would be feeling if you gave it up to him and he still left."

"If I would've done it, maybe he wouldn't be gone," she said, unsure.

"*Maybe* is the key word there. The uncertainty of it all is enough for you to send him packing."

"You're so strong, Payton. I don't know if I can do that."

"Remember, Rain, I wasn't strong initially. One thing I have learned is that guys come and go, circumstances come and go, but God is constant, and He can see you through all of this. The reason you didn't have sex with Tyson is that God wanted you to say no. Because you have honored Him, God is going to bless you. Yes, Tyson was the guy you loved, but you love God more and the Lord ain't gonna leave you.

13

He's gonna fix this. Just watch. Please, just don't make the mistake I made. If God sends you a good Christian guy, don't make him second best. You're gonna get over this, Rain. You have to pray and let God be your everything. You know I'm here for you. It's too bad you didn't bring clothes. You could have spent the night."

"We just got back from my grandmother's, and we brought her with us. I think I need to spend some time with her. Thanks for being such a great friend. I love you, Payton Skky. I used to think you were selfish sometimes and only cared about yourself, but I was wrong."

"I wasn't always a good friend, but I'm trying to be a better person. I'm trying to live like Jesus would and not like Payton would. You know what I'm sayin'?"

"Yeah, that's good advice, and I need to do that too. I know these next couple of days aren't going to be easy, but before I go tell me what's up with you, Payton. What's up with you and Georgia?"

"My school is a totally different place than I was used to. When I get down, I just think about high school and I laugh. Something about you, Dymond, or Lynzi always gets my spirit up. I had a roommate who tried to kill herself, two girls who wanted Tad and Dakari, a suite mate that didn't like me, bad grades, and a whole bunch of stuff."

"Oh, girl, are we gonna make it? College is hard."

"Yes, it is, but we made it through high school at Lucy Laney and you know how crazy that place was. We can make it, right?" I questioned.

"Yeah! I miss you, Payton."

"Girl, I miss you too."

"Granddaddy?" I said in a startled tone when I awoke from sleep and saw my grandfather standing over me.

It was Christmas morning, but the sun wasn't up yet. I heard heavy breathing and something made me wake up.

"Granddaddy, are you OK?"

"Yeah. I just thought I would get up early and maximize my day. It's Christmas, you know. I remember when I was your age. It was my first Christmas out of high school when I proposed to your grandmother."

"Right out of high school?"

"We didn't have choices about college back then. When you graduated you were considered an adult. I asked her to marry me, but what other choice could she make? As you guys say, I was *the man* back then and my game was tight."

I couldn't believe I was laughing at 5:10 in the morning. Something about being with him right then and there didn't bother me. I didn't care that it was early. I didn't care that I needed more sleep. I was just happy that he sat on the edge of my bed and told me romantic stories of him dating my grandmother.

"She was a great gal, Payton, and similar to you. She is beautiful now, but back then she made my heart dance."

"Oh, that's so sweet."

"What about you? Is your heart dancing for anybody? I've been praying for your mate."

"Are you trying to marry me off?" I joked. "Times have changed, Granddaddy. I'm not trying to get married until who-knows-when."

"That's good. I'm glad you're focused. Being an independent woman is great. But there is nothing wrong with letting a nice young gentleman into your life, especially the right one, one who loves the Lord. I don't want you to get with someone who looks halfway decent but treats you like he treats the bottom of his shoe. Be smart, my dear. You're my granddaughter, and you deserve the best. When I'm gone—"

"Don't say that," I said, cutting my grandfather off.

He had been talking about dying a lot lately, and it was starting to make me uncomfortable. I know no one can live forever, but just because he was old didn't mean he was going to go before me. I hugged him tightly. How dare he talk about when he was gone? He was so strong he was probably going to outlive all of us.

"Do you smell them biscuits?" he asked. "That's one thing I love about your grandmother."

My grandmother was up cooking early Christmas morning, and I knew my mother wouldn't like that too much. The whole point of staying at our house on Christmas morning was so that my mom could prepare her spread in her kitchen. Just like my grandmother wasn't too fond of Pillar's mom because she is white, she never really liked my mother, either, and my mother is black.

My grandmother and my mom didn't have a bad relationship, but it wasn't a warm and fuzzy one. So I got up, put on my robe, helped my grandfather into the kitchen, and went to find my mother to do damage control.

I hugged her and said, "Grandma is helping you out so you won't have to work so hard on Christmas."

"Don't tell me she's in there baking," my mom said with a slight attitude.

"All right, I won't," I told her.

She gave my dad a sour look. "Perry, you know I wanted to do this. Why didn't you tell your mother?"

"You know my mom," Dad said, throwing his hands up in the air.

It was Christmas morning, and I didn't want any family drama. "Let's all take a deep breath," I said, "and remember this is supposed to be a good day."

"Yeah, honey, just tolerate my mom for today. You know she doesn't mean any harm. She never does."

My mom was extremely disappointed, probably more so because her parents decided once again not to come to

Christmas dinner. My maternal grandparents lived in south Florida. She had no siblings so she missed her parents terribly. My mom had an older sister who had died from scarlet fever when she was ten, and her relationship with her mother was strained because of that. Maybe that was why Grandma couldn't really relate to me.

Today wasn't going like she wanted it to, and she needed a hug. So I followed her into her bathroom.

"Mom, I'm sorry your day isn't going like you planned. I just want you to know that Christmas can still be special and I love you. We can still celebrate Jesus' birth."

She grabbed my robe and pulled me toward her. "Thanks for understanding, Payton. Thanks for caring about me. But I will be fine. Now let me get ready and eat some of your grandmother's cooking. I prayed to Jesus because I didn't know how I was going to make it this morning, but He sent you in here to give me the wind to carry on. I'm glad you're home for the holidays. We will have to do something extra-special before you go back to school."

I went into the living room and grabbed a couple of presents from under the tree. My father had already given me an empty square box. Self-esteem was inside of it, he said. He told me I was just like the box, that I had self-esteem wrapped secretly inside. Every time I looked at the package I knew that we had that in common. I had been dealing with a lot last semester at school. I felt as if I didn't measure up, and my father's present made my day.

Now it was Christmas morning and I was ready to open some presents, put on some new clothes, get some money or something. As my dad always did, he went over and pulled out some old videotapes from Christmases past.

Perry Jr., my younger brother, came over to me with a present. "Here."

During all the Christmas rush I had forgotten to get him

17

something. I had something for everyone except him.

When I opened the present I saw a beautiful silver bracelet. "I'm gonna hook you up," I told him.

"You know what I want, right?"

Of course I knew. He wanted what he always wanted and what he could never seem to have enough of—tennis shoes.

Despite its rough beginning, we somehow got through the morning. My cousin Pillar and her family were supposed to come for Christmas, but they didn't. Though I missed Pillar, I wasn't heartbroken that she didn't come. My grandfather was really disappointed, but his two daughters were going to be there.

We arrived in Conyers about two, which gave my parents just enough time to get to the airport to pick up my two aunts. My Aunt Esther was coming from Dallas and my Aunt Georgia was coming from New Jersey.

As we ate a traditional soul-food dinner at my grandparents' table, I couldn't help but think about the Georgia football team. I hoped Tad was having a good Christmas.

Wow! I thought. *I'm not even thinking about Dakari, and he plays football, too. Lord, if there is any way You can help me get Tad back . . .*

My grandfather led most of the dinner conversation as he reminisced about his life. He talked about being a father of four kids and about getting the dealership.

"As I think back over all my years," my grandfather began, "life really started to get good for me at sixty. I finally went back to the place where I was born. God showed me that He wanted me to know Him, and that having a relationship with Him is far more important than anything. The Lord is my best friend. I'm going to leave here soon, but I know that I will have life eternally. Christmas Day is all about praising the name of Jesus Christ. When I leave this earth I can't wait for my Lord to say, 'Well done.' If God can't be enough to fulfill you, then what do you have to look forward to? Thank You, Jesus, for being good to me! Thank You," my grandfather shouted as he got up and left the table.

We all looked at one another. It wasn't a sermon, but it was a moving testimony.

My grandfather was right. Christmas was about praising the name of Jesus. The day was almost over, but before it was, my grandfather set us all straight about the true reason to celebrate Christmas.

Lord, I said on my knees in the guest room of my grandparents' home, *I feel so at peace right now and it feels as if You've come down from heaven and wrapped Your arms around me. Not that I'm wishing that wasn't the case, but something seems weird. I join my grandfather in praising You. Thank You for my blessing.*

My grandfather came into my room and cut my prayer short. "Payton, you make me so proud. Come and give me a hug."

I got off my knees and hugged my grandfather.

"Keep on doing what you're doing. Don't lose sight of the goal. It's all about winning souls for Him."

"I don't do a lot of witnessing, but Tad has helped me a lot."

"He sounds like a nice young man."

"I think you met him at graduation."

"Oh, I remember he was a really nice gentleman. Payton, I don't feel good. I'm going to go lie down for a while. Will you bring me some water in a little bit?"

"Yes. Of course I will, Granddaddy."

"Where did your dad go?"

"He went to play basketball with Perry."

"Where are all the ladies? The house is so quiet."

"They are out on the porch. Do you need any help?" I asked as I saw him cringe at his stomach.

"No, I'll be all right. You just make sure that everyone gets along and knows that it's Christmas."

I went into the kitchen to get my grandfather some water. It had been twenty minutes since I had talked to him. The heat wasn't on because the gas fireplace was going.

I opened the bedroom door and put the water on the dresser. He was asleep and it was cold in the house, but he didn't have a blanket on him. I got a blanket from the closet and tucked it around him. It was as if he was a block of ice. I picked up the glass of water and tried to wake him.

"Papa," I said softly, "wake up and drink some water."

I went to the other side of the room and turned on the light. He was lying almost too still and I started to panic.

"Papa, wake up."

I touched his chest. His heart wasn't beating. Without a thought I let go of the glass of water and started trying to make his heart beat with my hands.

I screamed, "Papa! Wake up!"

I heard the back door open and my brother and father laughing.

"Daddy! Come here! Hurry! It's Granddaddy!"

My father rushed into the room and Perry pulled me back. My father checked Granddad's pulse. "Call 911!"

"Oh, no," I screamed.

My screams alerted everyone. As they came into the room they realized what was going on and more cries started.

My dad turned to us and said, "He's gone." His eyes were bloodshot and I know it was hard for him to say.

I rushed to his side and buried my head in my grandfather's lap.

The paramedics finally arrived and my dad pulled me

away.

"No! Leave me alone!" I shouted.

"Payton, c'mon, honey. If anything can be done, let them do it."

I walked back to the doorway and stared at my grandfather. He had a look on his face that was happier than I had ever seen him. No one was touching me, but I felt that feeling again like when I fell on my knees. It was as if God was holding me. I realized why He had come earlier to give me peace. He knew I needed comfort that only He could give.

My grandfather was now with our heavenly Father, but I was really going to miss him. For that reason, it was hard embracing the good.

2

Releasing All Fears

*H*e was dead. Granddaddy was gone. Just as his heart had stopped beating, so did mine. Not for an eternity like his, but only for a second. However, that second felt like an eternity. I loved him so much because he taught me a lot. The thought of him not being at the head of our family anymore wasn't comforting.

Chaos was all around me. Paramedics were wheeling my grandfather's body from the house while another set of hands had to be called for my grandmother. It appeared as if she was having a stroke or a heart attack. My brother was so angry that he left the house in a fit of rage. My two aunts were crying uncontrollably. My parents were doing too much busy work, and it wasn't natural.

As I watched all of this, I stood as if I were a zombie. I realized I was scared. What would happen next? Papa was our rock. Now that he was gone, we were left to deal with the aftermath.

I should have gotten here sooner, I thought. *He asked me to bring him water. It's all my fault.*

No, came to my mind as if God was speaking to me. *It was his time. He told you to do something before he left. Do it, Payton. Do it.*

He asked me to bring him water, but I dropped that on the floor.

No, the voice stepped in, *something else he asked you to do. He asked you to try your best to keep the family together.*

That was my job. I had to tell everyone how happy he was in his last moments and how proud he was of us all. How my grandfather wanted us to continue victoriously until the day God called each and every one of us home.

I went to the bathroom and washed my face. The water refreshed my body and my soul. My grandfather wasn't there, but he was with Jesus, of that I was certain. It gave me hope because I didn't have to worry. The Lord knows how to take care of us better than anyone else. My grandfather was fine.

I went around the house trying to console everyone. I had strong arms for my aunts. They leaned on me, and I calmed them down. I checked with my grandmother, who was with the paramedics, and they said she was going to be OK. She didn't even need to go to the hospital; it was just shock. I held her hand as she fought the medicine that made her sleep.

"He's OK, Grandma. He was happy and God has him now."

When her eyes closed I went around the back of the house looking for my brother. He was out there shooting foul shots.

"It's not fair," he said when he noticed me standing behind him. "I didn't even get to say good-bye. I didn't get to tell him I love him. Why'd God have to take him out like that? Dang!"

"Who knows? There were a whole lot of things I wanted to do with Granddaddy, but we maximized his last hours here. He sat up and watched videos with us last night. We spent Christmas together. Though Christmas isn't the day I would have picked for Granddaddy to die, it helped that the family was together and we were able to lean on one another 'cause Granddaddy is OK."

"What are you talking about?" Perry asked as he threw the basketball down on the ground.

"Because he accepted Jesus, we know that Granddaddy will live with Him eternally. There is another life for him, a better life."

"Do you really think there is life after death?" he asked.

"Absolutely."

"C'mon, Payton. I believe in God and all, but we're about to see Granddaddy put into the ground. There is nothing appealing about dying. What do I have to give me hope that what you're saying is true?"

"Faith. When Granddaddy had his stroke a while back God could have taken him then, but He didn't. He gave us more time with him. There is Someone up there who cares about us, and all we have to do is believe and we can have everlasting life. We don't have to stress about it. Heaven is a wonderful place. I don't think I'm ready to go tonight, but if He calls, I'll go running. Granddaddy once told me that the only reason we are here is to get people fired up about going to heaven. I want to witness more."

My brother smiled and sat down by the basketball.

Lord, give me the words to minister to him and every other nonbeliever. I'm not used to witnessing, but I'm ready to be used by You.

"Payton, people are going to be coming over and I need you to clean up," my mom said, giving orders as soon as I walked back into the house.

I went over to my mother, grabbed her hands, and held them firmly. She was hurting and she didn't even realize it. My grandfather loved her like one of his own daughters.

Tears streamed gently down her face. "I'll miss him."

"I know, Mom," I told her. "So will I."

I wanted to help my dad deal with his father's passing, but he was at the store so that when people came over they would have food other than Christmas stuff to snack on.

I couldn't go to sleep that night. I wanted desperately to talk to Tad. He had just gone through this. His grandmother passed away at his graduation. Maybe what got him through could help me and my family, but he was in Florida getting ready for the bowl game. I certainly didn't need to get him down with my sad news. Even if I did want to talk to him, I had no idea where he was staying.

It wasn't as if he had an obligation to get me through it. He was no longer my boyfriend. I tried calling my girlfriends Lynzi, Rain, and Dymond, but all I got were answering machines. I thought about calling Laurel my college roommate, because she lived in Conyers, but it was too late. I would call her the next day.

I sat alone with my pillow, rocking myself back and forth. I was hurting, but I was trying not to make too much of it. Somehow I fell asleep and must have gone through the next couple of days in that same daze.

It was the last time I'd get to see Granddaddy. He still had that happy smile on his face. They were about to close the casket and my insides were turning. I felt uncomfortable. I felt scared. I felt weak because my grandfather just wasn't here anymore.

My brother, Perry, held my right hand while my cousin Pillar held my left.

25

"You don't have to worry about him. He's OK," Pillar said, trying to give me comfort as a tear trickled down her face.

"Thanks," I told her softly as I gripped her hand harder.

My grandfather had so many people who loved him. It took everything to hold my head up. I saw Dymond, Rain, and Lynzi, seated in the back. Seeing them gave me strength. I also saw Laurel and her father in the audience. All of my friends had blessed me with their presence. It felt as if my grandfather was telling me I didn't have to be afraid.

An hour later, when my grandfather's body was physically placed in the ground, I prayed. *Thank You, Lord, for my grandfather's faith in You. He was an awesome man. Because of his love for You, most of his children and grandchildren love You too.*

As I looked around and saw all the people, I knew my grandfather had left a great mark on this side of heaven. I could only hope that when it was my time to go, my life could be as fulfilling.

"Oh, so he wanted *you* to be over the estate," my Uncle Percy yelled to my father. My aunts were pretty angry, too, and my grandmother wasn't smiling.

My grandfather had left my father, the younger of his two sons, to oversee his estate. Upon my grandfather's retirement he had about a quarter of a million left to take care of. What my dad tried to explain to his siblings was that none of them lived close enough to help with any of his investments. This wasn't money my dad was going to put into his bank account.

"That's not true," my Uncle Percy continued. "Your way of thinking is all wrong. I could sell the rental properties and the money could be split among the four of us."

"What about me?" my grandmother piped up. "Shouldn't

it be split five ways?"

"No, Ma, I'm thinking four," Percy said. "Perry already has the car dealership in Augusta; he doesn't need any of this."

It was becoming a mess. My granddad hadn't been buried two days and they could hardly get along. I had to get out of there. My friend Laurel had told me she wanted me to spend the night at her house sometime. I didn't know if tonight would be a good time, but dealing with all this drama made me reconsider in a hurry.

I wanted to hang out with Pillar, but she, my aunt, and Pillar's brother flew back the night of the funeral.

"Laurel?" I said through the receiver as a sweet voice said hello.

"No, this is her mother. Payton?"

I was surprised that she recognized my voice and a little disappointed with myself that I didn't know Laurel's.

"How are you, honey? We've been praying for you and your family."

"Thank you, Mrs. Shadrach. I'm fine and I know my grandfather's in a better place."

"Hold on one second while I get Laurel."

Moments later Laurel came to the phone. "Hey, Payton. When are you coming to stay with me?"

"If you're not busy I would love to come over tonight."

"That would be great. Some of my girlfriends are coming over to watch a movie."

I said "OK, I'll see you later."

When Perry dropped me off at her house, Laurel wouldn't let him leave. She wanted him to come in and talk to her three brothers. Perry was hesitant about meeting them, but being that the NFL playoffs were on and my grandparents didn't have cable, he jumped at the opportunity when Laurel said they were watching it.

"Hey, guys," Laurel called out to her brothers, Lance, Liam, and Luke, "this is my roommate Payton and her brother, Perry."

"Hey," they all chimed back without taking their eyes off the television.

My brother plopped down on the couch as if he'd known them forever. "What's the score?"

"It's tied seven to seven going into the third quarter," Lance, her middle brother answered.

Perry responded, "Oh, it's a good game!"

"C'mon," Laurel said to me.

She took me upstairs to meet one of her friends. I was surprised to see a black chick sitting in her room with her arms out ready to give me a hug.

"Payton, I've heard so much about you. I'm Robyn."

"My other girlfriends, Brittany and Meagan, are coming by later," Laurel said to me. "After the football game is over we can watch TV downstairs. Do you want something to drink?"

"Yeah, whatever you have is fine with me," I told her.

Laurel left us alone and shut the door. I didn't know how to act around Robyn. I wasn't sure if she was down or if she was one of those black girls who acted white.

"So what's up?" Robyn asked. "Do you really like Georgia? Being up there with all those white people?"

We both laughed.

She was cool and I could tell that she and I were going to get along fine. She graduated with Laurel, but before going there she attended Southwest DeKalb High School. She was now at Fort Valley State University.

"There is a girl at Georgia who went to Southwest."

"I think I know who you're talking about. If she is as fast now as she was then . . ."

"Yep, we're talking about the same girl. She tried talking to my ex-boyfriend."

"Oh, girl, stop," Robyn said.

Robyn told me that Fort Valley was a great school, but she had been partying and she ended up with a 3.6 grade point average.

"I'm thinking of transferring to Georgia. Is it cool up there?"

"Yeah, girl, it's nice, but it's different."

Laurel came back to the room and said, "Well, gosh, you two are all chummy. I thought you'd get along. There's the doorbell. I'd better get it."

Robyn said, "OK, brace yourself because these two chicks are not like Laurel. Especially Brittany—she's out the box."

Brittany came into the room and said, "Payton, your outfit is adorable. Laurel didn't tell me her roommate had this much style."

I could tell what Robyn was talking about.

"So, Payton, what do your parents do?"

Laurel answered for me. "Her dad owns a car dealership in Augusta."

"Oh, really? Wow!"

The other girl hadn't said a word. I remembered that her name was Meagan. They decided to show me around Conyers. We all piled into Brittany's car and headed to the Waffle House. It was so packed with teenagers that we had to order our food and wait in the parking lot.

"I know he is not coming over here," Robyn said as she tried to walk behind me.

"Who?"

Before she could explain, a fairly cute guy who looked sort of familiar said, "Hey, don't I know you? You go to Georgia and hang with Tad and Dakari."

That was weird.

"I'm Jackson. I'm on the team with them."

"Why aren't you in Florida?" I asked.

"I'm going down for the game, but I'm not playing."

Robyn hit me in the back. "Ouch!" I said.

"Robyn," he said.

"Hey, Jackson."

The two of them had something going on, but I couldn't tell what it was.

"You know her? Are y'all friends?" Jackson questioned.

"Yeah, we're friends through Laurel," I told him.

"Robyn, I heard you were coming to Georgia. Couldn't live without me, huh?" he said arrogantly.

"Don't flatter yourself," she responded, rolling her eyes.

When we got back to Laurel's house, Brittany and Meagan decided not to spend the night, but Robyn did. She, Laurel, and I had a blast talking about everything.

"Did Laurel tell you about her boyfriend, Branson, breaking up with her right before homecoming?" Robyn asked, eager to share juicy tidbits of gossip about our mutual friend.

"Homecoming?" I asked. "I thought it was prom." I gave Laurel a confused look. "Or did he break up with you twice?"

Laurel chuckled. "No, it was homecoming."

"And he took your best friend to the dance, so you had to go with your brother," I said. "I know I remember that."

"Now your on the right track," Robyn confirmed.

"She was a cheerleader, right?" I said, wanting to make sure I had all the facts straight. "Wendy Cartright or something like that."

Robyn and Laurel started laughing so hard they almost fell off the bed.

"Wendy Cartright was our physics teacher." Robyn giggled.

"The girl who went to homecoming with Branson was Brittany Cox," Laurel explained.

I stared at Laurel. "You don't mean the Brittany who was just here, do you?"

Robyn and Laurel nodded.

"And you're still speaking to the girl?"

Laurel shrugged. "We did go through a pretty rough time there for a while. But eventually I had to forgive her. That's what friends do. That's what Jesus did for me."

"True, true," Robyn said.

I knew the Lord had brought me some terrific friends—girls I could laugh with, be myself with, and also be serious with when there was something to be serious about.

Robyn told me that Jackson Reid was her high-school love and they had problems in their relationship so she called it off, but she still liked him.

"Is that why you're going to Georgia?" I asked.

"No. It's not that far from home, and with my mom traveling with her books I need to be closer to my little sister."

"What books?" I asked.

"Oh, my mom is a Christian author."

"Really? I'm a Christian and I love to read."

"Great, I'll have to hook you up with some of her books. Anyway, that's the reason I'm going."

"Yeah, right, girl," I said. "I've got two ex-boyfriends at Georgia. I know."

We laughed about so many things. Laurel didn't seem a bit out of place, nor did I with a brand-new person around. I had a great time and I knew that's what my grandfather wanted me to do. I could only hope my relatives had solved their problems.

———————

Because my parents were going to be in Conyers for the rest of my vacation, Laurel and I had been hanging pretty tight. When she wasn't available, Robyn played hostess and spent time with me.

Though I hadn't heard from Tad, something told me to check my messages, and to my surprise he was on my machine.

"Payton, hey, it's me. I was just calling to see if you were OK. I hope things are getting better for you and your family. I still have those bowl tickets. I'll leave them at the front desk of the hotel. Come if you want them. They'll be waiting."

"What are you smiling about?" Robyn asked.

31

"Nothing. I didn't think he would call. It's no big deal."

"You didn't think who would call?"

"Tad, but it's no big deal."

We were eating Chinese food when Robyn asked, "What's going on?"

"I want to go to the bowl game, but I'm not sure if I can. My dad probably won't come."

"Well, I'll be there and I'm sure Laurel will want to come also."

"That's a great idea, but how are we going to get there?" I asked.

"Jackson's parents are going and they have an eighteen-passenger van. I'm sure we can ride with them," she suggested.

I never called Tad, although two days later I was in the van with Jackson and his parents, and we were headed to Orlando.

"Do you think Tad knows you're coming?" Laurel asked.

"I don't know," I told her. "Why in the world are Jackson's parents white?"

"Those are his foster parents. They really love him a lot and would do anything for him. Jackson feels the same way about them."

We were an hour away from Orlando, but we couldn't wait to eat so we stopped at Shoney's. The only problem was, I couldn't find my shoes. Jackson volunteered to stay and help me.

When I ducked my head to search under the seat I felt his hand touch my hair.

"What are you doing?" I asked harshly.

"I couldn't resist you and wanted to check you out."

"Don't touch me again."

"Don't come off like that. You know you liked it," he said as he put his arm around me. "Why you tryin' to play me? You know you like me. We can do this 'cause Robyn ain't my girl."

"What are you talking about?" I asked. I pushed him back quickly.

Before I made it into Shoney's, with one shoe on and one off, he grabbed my hand and said, "Don't say anything about this."

"First of all, don't be givin' me orders. Second, take your hands off me." I walked into the restaurant like nothing happened.

When we dropped Jackson off at his hotel, relief ran through my body. He was disgusting, and I was glad when he got out of the van.

We headed straight to Disney World in order to maximize our time in Florida. All the little children were happy to see the cartoon characters come to life. It reminded me of when I was young and my world was perfect. But now my Mickey Mouse days were gone.

"Thinking about something?" Laurel asked.

"Just taking life seriously."

"Don't take it too seriously or, before you know it, it will be gone."

"I know. I just want to make sure my life pleases God."

"That's great, Payton. God knows your heart, and He'll help you. Why don't we pray?" Laurel grabbed my hands and prayed, "Father, I ask You to bless Payton. Give her peace. We thank You for the forthcoming semester. Help us be a light to others. And selfishly I pray in the dating area. Help us there too."

I couldn't help but smile. The end of Laurel's prayer was silly, and I was truly thankful for a friend like her.

———

We were sitting in the stands watching the bowl game and Georgia was getting creamed by Michigan. It was the fourth quarter and the score was 0–30. Tad hadn't been in the game. The other running back was getting all the playing time and losing for us horribly.

Finally, with three minutes left, the coach put Tad in the game. I screamed louder than anyone in the place when Tad ran forty-seven yards with the ball. When he got the ball a second time, he ran fifty-six yards and scored a touchdown.

Unfortunately we still lost 7–30, so there wasn't much to celebrate. But we headed down to where the football team was anyway.

"I can't wait to meet him," Robyn said.

My heart skipped a beat when Tad walked out of the locker room, but before I could get to him I was cut off by a girl wearing one of those football hostess outfits. It was Vonda. The hug he gave her deflated my joy. What was I thinking?

"You should at least say hello," Laurel said.

"I don't want to."

"Tad!" Robyn called out.

He came over to me and said, "How have you been?"

"OK. I've been in Conyers. My grandfather passed," I said as my eyes started tearing up.

He pulled me to him. No one embraced me like Tad did. In the midst of all he had going on, he put his world aside and truly felt my pain. We were both there crying, and I felt as if I was releasing all fears.

3

Transitioning Once Again

*A*s I let go of my anguish in Tad's arms, I started to smile inwardly. I too had started to believe that things would be OK. I knew Robyn, Laurel, and a whole bunch of strangers were watching, but I didn't care. I guess Tad didn't, either, because he wasn't making a move to let me go.

Then a sarcastic voice screeched, "Time to go, Tad honey."

I didn't even have to look up to know who it was. Wherever Tad was going Vonda was going too. It was obvious that their relationship had gone further than I wanted to admit to myself.

When I saw her coming, I let go of him real fast. No sooner had I let go of him than Vonda grabed his hand and escorted him out of the tunnel. Tad didn't even say good-bye. He just threw up his hand and waved, which felt impersonal. I hated what was happening with us because nothing was happening. It was my fault because I chose to let him go. How stupid was I? Vonda was clearly making me see that I had made the wrong choice.

I assumed Tad must have been enjoying their relationship because he wasn't putting up a fight to be with me, nor did he let go of her hand. A brother isn't really into showing affection in public unless he really likes a woman.

"Dang it!" I shouted as I stomped my feet.

Laurel and Robyn came over and Robyn put her arm around me. "Your ex-boyfriend is really cute, but I see I'm not the only one who thinks that way."

"You got that right," I mumbled.

"Girl, don't worry about it. If he is supposed to be with you he will come back. Believe it. That's what Jackson and I are going through."

That didn't make me feel any better, especially with the way Jackson had been flirting with me earlier in the trip, but I had heard what she said somewhere before. It was my old principal Dr. Franklin when I caught Dakari with Starr. He told me to let Dakari go and if he was the one he would come back. If he didn't come back then I didn't need him anyway. I missed Dr. Franklin. I would have to go back to see him.

Dr. Franklin was right. Dakari did come back, even though he wasn't the one for me. Maybe I would try that approach with Tad. Even though we weren't a couple anymore, I still had feelings for him. I stood there watching him and Vonda leave the tunnel until I couldn't see them anymore. Though I was strong in stature, I was breaking inside.

Lord, help me, I said silently. *I miss Tad Taylor.*

The three of us turned to find Jackson's parents.

"There's Dakari," Laurel called out as she pointed to the bus.

I looked at Dakari, and he looked at me. He stared as if he could read my thoughts. He could tell my heart was with another, even though that guy didn't want my heart. What a weird triangle it had been for a year and a half. Nothing had changed; it had just gotten crazier.

36

Dakari said nothing to me. He just turned his head and got onto the bus. He was as sad over me as I was over Tad. I knew I was definitely over Dakari Ross Graham. For the longest time, when he needed me or wanted me to be there, I was there quicker than a heartbeat. However, I could not be this time. It was because of him that I had let Tad down in the first place. I wasn't blaming Dakari, but he had confused me, with his stuff. One minute he would want to be with me, only to break up with me all over again. All Dakari wanted was a physical relationship, but that's not something I would ever have with him.

"Are you OK?" Laurel asked.

"We lost the game; how can I be OK?" I said, laughing. "No, really, I am OK."

"Let's go find Jackson's parents," Robyn said.

"Yeah, the sooner the better," Laurel added, "because I'm hungry."

"And I'm ready to go home," I said.

———————

A week had passed and I was back in my cozy dorm room. I was there a day early, but it was OK because I had my car.

There was a knock on my door and when I opened it I saw Judy, our resident director.

"Well, Happy New Year, Payton. I was just checking to see if it was you. Not too many people are here."

"There's somebody on the other side of the bathroom," I told her, knowing I had heard commotion over there earlier.

"Yeah, it's Anna and her mother getting all of her stuff."

"What do you mean?"

Judy explained, "She's not going to school this semester. She's staying home."

"She's dropping out?" I asked as I ran into Anna's room.

I was too late. No one was there, and her bed was empty. I opened the closet to find all of her clothes gone.

Judy followed me in. "I wonder how many calls I'm going to get from girls wanting this room."

We had the nicest freshman dorm on campus, and being on the first floor did have its advantages.

"I wanted to say good-bye," I commented in a daze, not really caring about what Judy said.

"Maybe you can catch them in the parking lot."

"Yeah, maybe I can," I said, sprinting outside without any shoes on. "Anna! Anna, wait!"

"Payton," Anna said happily.

I was glad I caught her. We smiled at each other. She looked great.

"This is Payton?" her mom asked sweetly.

"Yes, Mom, this is her."

"Payton Skky, thank you so much," the lady said, throwing her arms around me. "Thank you for saving my Anna that night."

My semester had been crazy. My suite mate, Anna, tried to kill herself in our bathtub. I remember the night as if it was yesterday. I can still see the water seeping through the bottom of the bathroom door. My carpet was starting to get soggy and I heard the water running for what seemed like an eternity. Anna had taken too many pills and passed out. I called the paramedics, who were able to revive her. I guess I understood why she needed time, but I was going to miss her.

"You're welcome," I said to her mom.

"If it wasn't for you . . . who knows what would have happened to my Anna."

"I'm just happy God woke me up and allowed me to realize what had happened."

"Yes, you were definitely an angel that night. I was never really a believer before, but now I am."

"Me too," Anna said. "Please tell Jewels and Laurel that I plan to see them in the fall."

"We will all miss you so much."

"I'm not sure if Jewels will miss me. She will be too happy to have the room to herself."

"Well, she's gonna be sadly disappointed because Judy told me there is a list for the room a mile long. I'm just sad that we have to replace you. But there's no way that's going to happen. You've grown on me, girl."

"Payton, dear, you don't even have any shoes on," her mother said.

"Yeah, I guess I'd better get in and let you guys go."

"Payton," Anna said, "I have your number, and I'll give you a call."

"I have your number at home and I've been meaning to call, but I guess you can't always wait until tomorrow . . ."

Anna finished my statement by saying, "Yep, 'cause tomorrow may not come. But I'll be back."

We hugged.

"It's going to be hard for me, not being in school."

"Well, it's going to be hard for me to come back. My grades were not all that great last semester."

"Study hard for the both of us and I'll rest enough for the both of us. You just get those good grades. You can do it. After all, you saved my life. I'm sure you can get a lousy A."

We both chuckled.

"It was very nice meeting you," I said to her mother.

"You too, dear," she responded.

"And thanks for the flowers you sent to my house. You didn't have to do that," I said.

"We just wanted to show you that we appreciate what you did for Anna. I can never say it enough. I remember when the girl from your dorm was found dead and I imagined her parents getting that phone call. I was thankful that when I got the call it had a happier ending."

We said good-bye five more times before I went inside, changed my socks, and stretched out on the bed.

Last semester was not what I thought it should be. A girl in our dorm went out on a blind date and was killed. I hoped this semester would be a lot less dramatic.

I had promised myself and the Lord that this semester would be different. I decided that I wasn't going to lack confidence in myself like I did my first semester.

I got up very early to have some quiet time with God. I wanted to pray to Him, write in my journal, and read His Word. After I had spent twenty minutes being spiritually filled, I heard a whole bunch of commotion going on from the other side of the bathroom. It didn't take long to figure out who it had to be. Jewels was back.

It wasn't even light outside and she already had the music blasting. I wasn't ready for her return. By the end of the first semester I was barely used to her ways, and now it was apparent that I had no choice but to get used to them.

"Lord," I said with quite a bit of frustration, "I don't really like Jewels and I wish it was her that didn't return. I know that's not the way You want me to be, so I'm praying for You to intervene so I can tolerate Goody Two-shoes Miss Jewels."

No sooner had I finished praying than my door opened and Laurel entered. I had just hung out with her a week ago, but I missed her. Just seeing her warm face took away all the negative thoughts harboring inside me. We reached out and hugged each other as if we were sisters.

I was about to shut the door behind Laurel when she said, "Wait! My dad is coming."

"So what have you been up to?" I asked, yelling over the music.

"I can't hear you!" she yelled back.

Her father walked in and said, "This music is too loud. Where is it coming from?"

I pointed to our bathroom.

He set Laurel's suitcases down and went into Jewels's room.

She was dancing and putting her clothes away so she didn't notice Laurel's father when he entered. He went over to the radio and turned it down.

"Who is that touching my radio?" she yelled.

When she saw Reverend Shadrach she acted like a totally different person I had never had the pleasure of meeting. She acted sweet and innocent and apologized to him over and over.

I said to myself, *Ain't this a trip? She's gonna try and act like she is sweet.*

Laurel's father came back to our room and shut the bathroom door, "Well, Laurel, I remember when I dropped you off the first time five months ago. I see you girls survived as roommates. I'll be continuing to pray that things go well for both of you here at Georgia. Lean on each other."

"Oh, Dad, I'm going to miss you," Laurel said as she hugged her father.

Her dad replied, "I'll miss you, too, sweetie."

"Good-bye, sir," I said as he left our room.

"Did you get all the classes you wanted?" I asked Laurel, referring to our schedules we received in the mail.

"Yeah. I don't have to do anything as far as registration, but I wanted to come and get settled. When did you get here?" she asked.

"Yesterday afternoon."

"What have you been doing?"

"Meditating, I guess."

There was a quick knock on the bathroom door before it opened. I hated the fact that there were no locks on the door between Jewels's room and ours.

"Why are you looking at me like that, Payton? All you guys had to do was tell me that my music was too loud and I would've turned it down. You didn't have to tell your dad to get on me. This isn't elementary, you know."

"Jewels," Laurel said, "my dad heard your music himself and he called you, but you didn't answer so he did what he had to do."

"I was just taking advantage of my time before my roommate came back. Now that I know you guys can't appreciate good music, you don't have to worry about it being so—"

"So loud," I screamed at her to hurt her ears like her music had hurt mine. "Anyway, come in here a second, will you?"

"OK, Payton, but hurry up. The next song on the CD is my favorite."

"Jewels, it's a CD. You can play the song one hundred times if you want to. This is important."

"What?"

"I saw Anna and her mother yesterday," I explained to them both as I sat on my bed. "She's not coming back this semester. She's still trying to sort out what happened. She wants to enroll again in the fall."

Laurel sat on her bed. The news I had given her had deflated her spirit. I looked up at Jewels and even she was disappointed.

For the first time we put aside our differences and our feelings to come together to help one another get through. We all admitted that every time we took a shower or a bath Anna's tragedy would come up. Laurel suggested that we pray in the bathroom for Anna, for us, and for every college student facing adversity. Jewels wasn't a Christian, but she didn't really object to prayer.

God says if you lift Him up He will draw people closer to Him. I wondered if that was the case with Jewels. That was my cue. I knew then that I was going to start to minister to her on a regular basis and I was going to be committed to that.

At about five in the afternoon Laurel and I went to the cafeteria for dinner. We were waiting on Robyn because after that we were going to show her around campus. I wasn't too excited about doing that in the dark, but with the three of us together, I figured we'd be pretty safe.

As we were waiting on Robyn, Jewels entered our room all bubbly. Something had to be up. I wondered what it was.

"I'm so excited, you guys," she blurted. "Judy called me and none of the girls on the waiting list want my room."

"What do you mean, none of them want your room?" Laurel questioned with a look of disbelief.

I was confused too. Our dorm was close to campus and our commons area looked the best. Why no one wanted to move there baffled me.

"Judy said everyone turned it down because they knew Anna tried to . . . well, you know. They didn't want to sleep in the bed that someone so depressed slept in. They don't want to use the tub she tried to kill herself in. They still haven't been able to rent out Worth Zachary's room. Even the girl she roomed with moved out. I'm so excited. I get the room to myself."

A knock on the door interrupted Jewels's celebration. Laurel opened it, and Robyn gave her a big hug.

It was funny because she was so proper when she spoke to Laurel. "Hello. How have you been? I made it." She then came over to me and said, "What's up, girl? How you doin'? I'm at Georgia now."

It was so refreshing. I too was an African-American girl who could flip the switch. Just like turning the light on and off. I could be proper when I needed to, but I could be down as well.

The funny thing was that Laurel didn't even get the difference. However, Jewels did, and she looked at Robyn with eyes that asked, *Where in the world did she come from?*

Robyn stuck out her hand and said, "Hi, I'm Robyn."

Jewels coldly said, "Oh."

I grabbed my coat, put my arm through Robyn's, and escorted her out the door. She didn't need to think about fooling with Jewels and her snooty attitude.

When we got into the hallway she asked, "What was wrong with her?"

"Don't take it personally," Laurel explained. "She's like that with everybody."

Later that evening at dinner Robyn told us that her mother was staying at a nearby hotel in Athens. They were having problems finding her a room. She told Laurel and me that she didn't know where she was going to end up.

Laurel and I looked at each other in a weird way. My roommate and I were connecting. I knew we were thinking the same thought. Robyn could be our suite mate. She could stay with Jewels and it would be perfect.

"Are you thinking what I'm thinking, Payton?" Laurel asked.

"Yeah, tell her."

Laurel explained, "Our suite mate Anna isn't coming back, and her side of the room is free."

"That sounds great. I can be with you guys. Wait, does that mean I have to room with that girl? No."

I said, "Don't back down, Robyn. Maybe you are exactly what Jewels needs to understand that the world does not revolve around her."

"Payton, I'm here to get an education, not school somebody."

The more Laurel and I sold her on the idea the more

44

Robyn mirrored our ways. By the end of dinner she was psyched. Laurel had already told her about what Anna had done, but it didn't bother Robyn.

Before we got up from the table we held hands and prayed.

"Father," I led humbly, "we know that only You could have given us such a cool idea. Now that we are excited, we ask You to help make it happen. Jewels didn't want to share the bathroom with me because I am black and Robyn isn't any lighter, but maybe Robyn can change Jewels's ways. We ask You to make sure that You are the focal point, to keep You lifted high in our dorm spaces, to keep the evil, stress, strife, jealousy, and anger out. Lord, I pray for Jewels's heart. Help us to respond to her ignorant comments the way You would, not the way we would want to. Help Robyn in the transition, help Laurel to continue doing well, and help me to do better this semester. We love You and thank You. Amen."

After we got up from the table and put our trays away, we walked back to the dorm room. It was dark, but we had hope in our hearts. There were several obstacles in front of us, but we knew God was going to work things out. That kind of faith felt really good.

Lord, I thought, *I'm getting it. I understand this Christian walk thing. Thank You for taking me step by step and showing me the way. I trust You. I totally trust You.*

"OK, guys," I said as the three of us stood outside Judy's room, "I'll handle this."

"Payton, are you sure that's a good idea?" Laurel looked at me and asked with concern.

Judy definitely didn't owe me any favors. I was responsible for wrecking her car a few months back. I didn't hit it, but my friend Cammie had to drive because I was a little tipsy. I saw Dakari kissing another girl and I didn't want to feel the pain it had caused. After Cammie hit the car I told her not to say anything and I moved my car to another place. It took a lot to go to Judy and apologize, but she was cool about it.

When Judy opened the door I wanted to change my mind, but I spoke anyway. "Judy, can I talk to you, please?"

"Yeah. What's going on?"

"This is Robyn Williams. She went to high school with Laurel and she just transferred. The school is having problems finding Robyn a room and we were hoping she could room with Jewels."

Judy was silent for about fifteen seconds before she said, "Robyn, if you want it, it's yours. Payton and Laurel did disclose to you everything that happened, didn't they?"

"Yes," Robyn said, "they told me about what happened to the other girl. My mom is here in town. When can we take care of everything?"

"Tomorrow."

Having faith does work, huh, Lord? You worked it out just like I knew You would.

Next came the hurdle of telling Jewels. Just as we were going to our room I looked up and saw a sight that made me sweat. It was Tad Taylor.

"You guys go on to the room," I said, trying to get my girls to leave before they could see why I wanted to be detained.

I wasn't so lucky.

"Oh, it's Tad," Laurel said, teasing.

"Handle your business, girl," Robyn said. "We'll see you in the room, and I want details."

"Hey," Tad said, looking a little down.

"What's up?" I asked, having a calm mind and courageous spirit.

"Didn't you hear what's up?"

46

"No, I don't know what's going on. Tell me."

"They just fired our coach. I might leave this place. I was supposed to start this season."

"Tad, I'm sure the new coach will let you. Sure, Randall was in the bowl game, but look where that got us."

"Yeah, but the coach wouldn't put a freshman in the game," I commented, trying to figure it out.

"I don't think that's true."

"Coach Eckerd was going to let them know that next year was going to be different, but they didn't even give him a chance. What am I gonna do, Payton?"

I took his arm and led him outside. "Look," I told him, "you're the one who told me I needed to trust God more and I'm starting to do it. Don't you fall apart on me. Tad, I'm sorry about Coach Eckerd, but it wasn't guaranteed. The only thing that is guaranteed is that we, as Christians, are gonna be with the Lord one day. Nothing else matters."

He was hearing me, but yet he was pouting. He walked away from me and folded his arms. I walked over to him and stared in his eyes. "If God closed this door, He is gonna open another one. He has a plan for both you and Coach Eckerd. You've got to trust the Lord. What's wrong with a little competition, anyway?"

"I've done that all year long."

"So what? Look how much it helped you in a bowl game. You showed out."

"A lot of people were saying that was only because the second string was in for Michigan."

"The second string was in for a long time and nobody was doing anything on Georgia's team. It took you to come in and get things going. God's gonna make sure you don't go anywhere."

"How do you know?"

"I don't know how I know, but I do know it's going to get better."

"Yeah," he said, finally buying into what I had been saying. "God's going to make it better. Thanks, Payton."

He kissed me on the cheek and dashed away.

When I returned to my room Robyn was waiting for me. Laurel was in with Jewels and I could hear voices escalating. This wasn't going to be pretty.

"Look, she doesn't want to room with me, and after talking to her for five minutes I don't want to room with her either. She's crazy. Let's you and me room together and let the white folks room on the other side. It could be cool up in here, you know what I'm sayin'?"

"Robyn, I like you, but I'd miss Laurel a lot."

"You want to continue rooming with her?"

"Yeah, I do."

"Good," Laurel said as she overheard us in the bathroom. "Robyn, you and Jewels are just going to have to work it out."

"That's cool, but y'all get ready. She ain't gonna push me over the edge like she did that other girl."

We all laughed.

———————

A week later I had settled into my classes. Robyn and Jewels were fussing almost every hour, but I think they liked getting on each other's nerves. I was excited about having a car again. It was such a blessing. I gassed it up at the local BP and got in line for my new vehicle to be washed.

A man pulled up behind me and I noticed he had dropped his wallet at the pump. I got out of my car and tapped on his window. He smiled as he rolled it down.

"Sir, I'm sorry to bother you, but I saw you leave that pump and you dropped your wallet on the ground."

"Oh, thank you, young lady," he said as he stepped out of the car to retrieve his wallet. I returned to my car.

As I was opening my door he asked, "Are you a student here?"

"Yes."

"Hi. I'm Mike Randolph. I just accepted the position as head football coach here."

"Really? Wow! I know some guys on the team."

"Really? Who?"

"Dakari Graham and Tad Taylor."

"Yeah, that Tad Taylor has some talent."

"He sure does."

Lord, I prayed, *am I supposed to be putting in a good word for Tad? What am I going to say?*

"Have you met any of your players yet?" I asked.

"No, that's happening later this afternoon."

"I know I'm being forward, but Tad's a great athlete. He was promised that he would get to start. He's actually thinking about changing schools if he doesn't."

"From what I've seen on film, Tad Taylor definitely has potential. He's a fine running back, and I don't want to lose him. Thanks."

It was now my turn to go into the car wash. As the suds filled my view I got excited. My spirit had changed. God was now totally in control, and He was doing awesome things. I realized that for the better I was transitioning once again.

4

Learning What's Important

*I*t was the beginning of February and Athens was being hit by a severe ice storm. Classes were canceled and everyone was told to stay in their dorms or the library. At first I thought it was a joke, but then I thought it was a good idea. Being locked in the library would be great for me to get some studying done.

As soon as I opened the door to my dorm room I heard the sound of ice pellets hitting my window.

Gosh, I made it just in time.

No sooner had I put my stuff down than the phone rang. I knew it would be my mom calling to check in.

"Hey, Mom," I said before giving her a chance to say anything. "I'm all right."

"Well, I'm glad," the cool voice on the other end said, "but I'm not your mom."

"Tad Taylor!"

"Payton Skky," he replied.

"To what do I owe the honor?" I said as I dived onto my

bed and listened to his charming, husky voice.

"Thanks for talking to Coach for me."

"It was just a fluke that I met him," I explained to Tad.

"Why didn't you call me and give me the heads-up?"

"I don't know. I prayed for you, though. You had me worried the day you came over here."

"You must not have been too worried. You didn't call to check up on me."

"Would you have wanted me to? I thought that was what Vonda was for."

"Oh, so now you got jokes?"

"I'm not joking, I'm serious." I laughed. "What's up? Is that all you wanted?"

I could have talked to him for hours, yet I was rushing him off the phone. I wasn't allowing myself to get caught up and that was a blessing. I was moving forward with my life. I sat up on my bed and realized that I didn't need to trip because Tad called. We were friends and nothing more, and I needed to get used to that.

"Well, dang, since you're tryin' to get a brother off the phone and all, let me tell you why I called."

"OK, go ahead."

"So you are tryin' to get me off the phone since you ain't denying it."

"Oh, stop. What's going on?"

"Well, recruiting season is starting and there aren't that many black girls that are hostesses for football, and the coach thinks a few more would help. He wanted to know if you could help find some other girls to join."

I didn't mean to keep mentioning the girl in his life, but I wanted to know what he was getting himself into.

"Isn't Vonda in it? I saw her wearing the uniform."

"Yeah, but there are only five black girls and thirty-two white girls. So what do you say? Do you have time to squeeze it in?"

"I don't know. I was thinking about doing things with SGA, but those things go hand in hand."

"Do you think you can talk some girls into doing it?"

"I don't know that many black girls, but I'll talk to some folks. When is the meeting?"

"On Wednesday."

"Dang, Tad! It's already Monday."

"Don't even try it. You know you can hook it up and pull it together."

"What does a hostess do anyway? When I came up here with Dakari some of those girls were flirtin' and I'm not about that."

"I wouldn't tell you to do anything like that. Plus, every time a hostess is paired with a recruit, a football player goes with her. I'll make sure we are together."

"Do you think Vonda would like that?"

"Payton, Vonda doesn't trip over the small stuff."

Yeah, we'll see, I thought

"Sign me up," I told him. "This should be a lot of fun. I'll touch base with you tomorrow after I talk to my friends."

"Thanks, Pay. I'll see ya later."

"OK, bye."

After hanging up I went into the bathroom. I saw Robyn with her head in the sink, and she was crying. I was truly tired of my bathroom being a place of despair.

"Girl, what's wrong?"

She lifted her head from the sink and fell into my arms. She was sobbing uncontrollably.

"It's OK," I kept telling her, not having a clue what was going on. I hadn't seen Robyn much lately because all her time was spent with Jackson. Somehow they'd gotten back together. Since she seemed happy, I didn't bother telling her I thought he was a jerk. "What did Jackson do?" I asked after her tears subsided.

"I went to his apartment and there was a car parked in

his extra space. At first I thought it was one of his friends, but then I saw the Sigma Gamma Rho tag and I knew it had to be a girl. I went up and heard female laughter coming from his bedroom window and I saw him in bed with a girl. I started banging on the glass until he came out with a towel wrapped around him. The Negro didn't even have on any underwear so you know he was doing something."

"Girl, just be glad it wasn't you. If y'all had been sleeping together, this would have been harder to take."

"Payton, I'm not a virgin. Jackson and I are sexually active, but I'm on the pill. This is hard to say, but in high school last year I got pregnant by Jackson. I had an abortion. I told God I wouldn't do it anymore. I did try to stay pure after that, but I couldn't help it. I love Jackson and I left Fort Valley to be with him. I'm so stupid. You might as well change the spelling of my name from R-o-b-y-n to F-o-o-l."

Everything she told me was very heavy. This was some deep stuff. *Lord, what am I supposed to say?*

I sat on the floor by my bed and Robyn placed her head in my lap. As I stroked her hair I prayed. "Lord, we often fall as Christians. Right now I lift Robyn up. Her heart is shattered. It's because she has been out of Your will. I know somewhere Your Spirit is in there waiting to shine through. May her thoughts be pleasing to You. Help her not try to mend things with a guy who doesn't have her best interests at heart. Also I pray for Jackson that he can realize the only thing that is important is You, not how many women he can get. Just like You helped me, Lord, help Rob to know that what she feels for Jackson is not love. The men You have waiting for us would never lead us into so much sin. Lord, make Robyn know that I am here for her and that she can trust me. May the two of us get through this together. We love You and we praise You. In Jesus' name we pray. Amen."

"Thank you, Payton."

I pushed a few buttons on my CD player and we listened

to Donnie McClurkin's album. One song, "We Fall Down," stood out. We do fall down as Christians, but we get up with Christ. I was trying to get up in my life. My perspective on things was changing. I was truly growing, and I didn't want that to end. Every day I was going to be more like Christ.

"Should we be watching this movie? It's lightning really bad, you guys," I said to Robyn and Laurel.

We were watching a comedy and I was laughing hysterically. Even Robyn was laughing, but something was wrong with Laurel.

"Laurel, what's wrong? You don't seem like yourself," I said.

Snapping, Laurel replied, "Can't I just watch the movie without laughing at every dumb comment?"

Robyn looked up from the floor and said, "Dang! You PMS-in' or what?"

"Just leave me alone, guys. Payton, you always want to fix everything. I don't need that right now." Laurel got up from the bed and went into the bathroom.

"What's up with her?" Robyn asked.

"I tried to find out, but she doesn't want to tell me."

"She's been hangin' around with Jewels too long, that's what's up," Robyn joked. "They just don't know they can't go off on a sista like that. Sistas don't play that."

"I know that's right, but Laurel's cool," I defended.

"Yeah, Laurel's cool, but that was rude."

"She's never rude like that. Something is goin' on. I know I can't fix everything, but she's been there for me. I'm gonna pray for her, and I'm definitely not gonna let it stress me out. You know what I'm sayin'?"

Robyn gave me five and we continued watching the movie. Laurel came out of the bathroom and apologized. I didn't pray with her, but I prayed for her. It was a long night, but the rain and ice finally stopped. Robyn returned to her room and we went to sleep.

Before Robyn and I watched the movie with Laurel, Robyn talked extensively to me about transferring back to Fort Valley. She said she didn't think she had a reason to stay anymore since she and Jackson had unofficially broken up. That's when I told her about becoming a Georgia Girl. This school had so many other things to offer besides Jackson. She was excited and promised to help me find other black girls to help us.

I liked Robyn. She had loyalty. I hadn't seen my friends from last semester—Cammie, Blake, and Shanay—but I needed to find them to ask them about being Georgia Girls.

Robyn and I were sharing an umbrella as we walked to class on Tuesday morning.

"Payton Skky," someone said to me, "is that you?"

I turned around and was stunned to see Summer Love in front of me. "Girl, how have you been?" Last time I had seen her was at the debutante ball. Though she was from my hometown, she and I didn't hang with the same crowd so I never ran into her. "You're doing gymnastics, right?" I asked her.

"Yeah. I was actually worried about my spot on the team, but I worked hard and I beat another girl out."

"The other girl who didn't make the team, was her name Laurel? That's my roommate."

I couldn't believe this. There had to be a mistake. There was no way Laurel could be off the gymnastics team. Clearly that couldn't be what I heard. It made perfect sense, however. That would explain Laurel's bad attitude.

Summer went on to explain everything. They asked Laurel to stick around and be equipment manager, but that was something she wasn't into. Gymnastics was her whole life.

"I think I do remember Laurel telling me that her room-mate was from Augusta," Summer said "We've got to hang out sometime."

"Yeah," I said in a deflated tone. "This is my friend Robyn."

Summer and I exchanged numbers and Robyn and I went to class.

"I hate that for Laurel," Robyn said.

"Yeah, me too. What is this, 'meet everybody you know on the block' day?" I joked to Robyn as Shanay and Blake came up to me.

"Hey, Payton. Happy New Year, girl," Blake said.

"Hey, y'all. This is Robyn. Robyn, this is Blake and Shanay."

Shanay said, "Robyn Williams, what are you doing here, girrrl? I heard you went to Fort Valley. Since you moved to Conyers with the white folks it seems you missed them and came up here to Georgia, huh?"

"Ha, ha, ha," Robyn said sarcastically.

"For real, though. How have you been?" asked Shanay.

"I'm cool."

"I was gonna call y'all because we need some hostesses for the football team," I said.

When Shanay and Blake looked at each other with big eyes and wide smiles, I knew they were down with being Georgia Girls.

"We have a meeting tomorrow. Come to my dorm at 4:30 and we can walk over together."

Robyn and I went to our English classes. We didn't have the same class, but they were right around the corner from each other. As we tried to put down the umbrella, I clumsily dropped my books. When I looked up, I had help.

"Thanks," I said without looking at the person. When I did, I saw it was Cammie. "Hey, girl," I said, trying to give her a hug, but she jumped back.

"Don't try and hug me. You got new friends and didn't try to call me or nothin'." She was jealous of Robyn.

"Girl, I'm sorry. I've been so busy at school," I said.

"Payton, I'm not talkin' about school. I called you at home a lot during vacation, but you never returned my calls."

I sighed. "My grandfather passed and I was busy with family."

"Oh, I'm sorry, Payton. I didn't know," she said, hugging me.

"It's cool. This is Robyn. She lives in the same town as my grandmother. We're staying in the same dorm."

"Yeah, I'm Payton's suite mate," Robyn said.

I could tell Cammie was not too thrilled about someone besides her spending time with me.

"Hey, we're going to a Georgia Girl meeting. Do you want to come?"

"I could never be around football players," Cammie said, pointing to her waist. She was really self-conscious about her size.

"Don't worry, girl. I'm gonna come to your room tonight and hook you up," I told her.

As the three of us went our separate ways I realized how important friendships are. I didn't know what I was going to say to Laurel, but I knew God was going to help me through. She was off the team that she'd been working to be on her whole life. That was major.

"Laurel," I said with anxiety in my voice when I saw her head down on the desk.

"I'm fine," she told me.

"What do you mean, you're fine? I ran into Summer and she told me everything. You don't have to play tough."

"I was upset at first, but I've been studying the Word and I know God's got something for me. Gymnastics has been great, but maybe it's time to let go. I talked to Foster today."

"Who's Foster?"

"My ex-boyfriend. He's a good Christian guy who goes to USC."

"Why'd y'all break up?"

"I wasn't where he was spiritually and he wanted a more committed relationship and a stronger sister in Christ. Anyway, he let me know that I had more going on for me than gymnastics. God wants me to make sure the lost know Him. My priorities were so messed up," she told me.

"I've been praying for you all day."

"Thanks. God has been with me all day, and I know He will give me the desires of my heart."

"Laurel, I'm in the same place," I told her honestly.

"We should do a Bible study together," she suggested.

"I'm cool with that. Pick something out and let's get started."

"OK, I'll go to the Christian bookstore tomorrow. We can keep each other accountable."

"Maybe we can become young ladies that God is proud to call His own. I don't know how Summer beat you."

"She was better at floor and I was too stiff."

"You may be stiff, but you've got the best rhythm out there."

"How do you know?"

"Your heart beats for Jesus, and that's the only thing that matters."

"You're right," she said.

Laurel and I were realizing the same thing about God.

The Georgia Girls met in the football facility, which was nice.

"Hayli!" I said when I saw my old friend.

She turned and gave me a hug. "It's great that you're

gonna do this. You'll have so much fun."

"What are you doing here?" I asked.

"I'm trainin' y'all, girl. It's good to see you."

"How are the wedding plans coming?" I asked with a smile.

"The wedding plans are on hold. Drake and I want to follow different things in life. I want to follow God and he wants to follow his fame. He worships himself, and it's sad."

"That is sad, but I'm glad you're being strong."

"All right, ladies, I want to call this meeting to order," Mrs. Senator, the lady in charge, said.

I sat beside Robyn, Shanay, Blake, and Cammie. Cammie looked cute after our makeover.

The meeting lasted an hour and we were measured for our uniforms. The first recruits were coming on Friday. All five of us were excited. I was glad Tad asked me to do it. When I thought of him I looked around for Vonda and was glad when I didn't see her.

Whatever comes in life, Christ can get you through it. I was definitely a better person this year. I was getting a hold on things. I was learning what's important.

5

Building
on History

H ey, girl," I said with excitement as Rain answered her phone.

"Is that you, Payton?"

"Yeah, it's me."

"What are you doin' callin' me on a Thursday night?"

"I can't call you now that you're in college?"

"Yeah, it's just that I haven't heard from you in a while. I can barely hear you now. Where are you?"

"Girl, I'm outside walkin' to a meeting. It's dark, and I don't need to be alone. I just thought I would check in on you."

"That's good, but I should be askin' how you are. I just lost a stupid boyfriend, but you lost your grandfather. Are you all right? How are you holdin' up?"

"Actually I'm all right."

"That's good. And your family?"

"Everybody's good, but I haven't heard from them. You know how that goes."

"Yep, I feel you."

"So Rain, what's up with you? Are you able to survive without Tyson?"

"It was hard at first, but then my Morehouse brother started being really nice to me."

"Your Morehouse brother? What's that?"

"When you first come to Spelman they match you up with a brother at Morehouse. You're supposed to help each other get adjusted and stuff. Anyway, mine is so cute. He's from Dallas and he likes me. We're takin' it slow, but he let me know that Tyson is not the only brother out there. How come I'm doin' a Payton Skky?"

"What are you talkin' about?" I questioned.

"He plays basketball just like Tyson. All your men play football. Why all my men gotta play basketball?"

"That's 'cause you tall, girl. Not that your boyfriend has to be taller than you, but you know you like them tall and skinny."

"Oh, you got jokes, huh?"

"Girl, I miss you."

"Yeah, I miss you, too, Payton. Have you talked to Dymond or Lynzi?"

"No, not yet. Maybe we should do a three-way soon."

"What are you doin' for spring break?" she asked.

"I don't have any plans. What about you?"

"I don't have any plans either. We're goin' to have to road trip somewhere," Rain suggested.

"Sounds good to me. I can't wait to meet this guy. I might have to stop down in Atlanta soon."

"Yeah, I want you to. I'll let you know when the basketball games start so you can come down with me."

"Cool. Well, I'm gonna let you go now. I'm almost to the building. You kept me safe," I said.

"Like I'd be able to do anything all the way in Atlanta."

"Just hearin' your voice made me feel safe. Big hug through

the phone!"

"Big hug back!" Rain exclaimed.

"See ya, Rain."

"'Bye," she said as I hung up the phone.

"Boo!" a familiar voice said all of a sudden, nearly scaring me to death.

"Dakari Graham!" I screamed, hitting him over the head with my purse. "You know you wrong!"

"You know you wrong, girl. Out here by yourself. I thought that was you walkin', swingin' them hips. I was supposed to be headin' back to the dorm, but you made me follow."

"Boy, I got this long coat on. You know you can't see nothin'."

He chuckled. "That's what you think."

"Move from in front of me."

It had been a while since I had talked to Dakari. I hadn't seen him since the bowl game, but we didn't speak then. I hadn't missed him one bit.

"What have you been up to, Payton?" he asked.

"Nothin' much."

"Where are you headin' to?"

"I'm goin' to a SGA meeting."

"Dang! You gettin' involved in politics?"

"You know I did it in high school," I reminded him.

"Yeah, but it's really political on this level."

"I know. Actually Hayli's the one who suggested I get involved."

"Hayli? That girl is takin' my brother through all kinds of changes. That's probably why y'all get along."

"Why you say that?"

"Don't trip. You know you took me through a whole bunch of changes."

"Whatever, Dakari!"

"Don't get mad. I'm just tellin' the truth."

"From what I hear, your brother can't even respect the fact that he's engaged."

I didn't want to go into serious detail with Dakari. My conversation with Hayli was strictly between us. Dakari had a big mouth anyway. He would probably go back and tell Drake.

"What you talkin' about? What do you know?" he asked, getting really defensive.

"Nothin'. I don't know a thing."

He kept persisting because he's stubborn, but I didn't have time for his foolishness.

"Dakari, get out of my way. I have a meeting to go to."

"You should thank me for makin' sure you got here safely. You know we got crazy people roamin' the campus."

"That's nice, scare me."

"I'm just tryin' to tell you to be smart. Go ahead and be hardheaded."

"No, you're right. Thanks, Dakari."

"So are we gonna get together soon? You know you missed me. You didn't even say nothin' about my Kobe Bryant hairstyle."

"It's cute."

"You like it, don't you?"

"Dakari." I sighed with aggravation.

"All right, I'ma call you though," he said before he quickly kissed me on the cheek and dashed around the corner.

He was so slick.

I must have gotten the meeting time wrong because when I got inside the building Karlton was already presiding over the meeting. He smiled at me and motioned for me to have a seat.

Karlton Kincaid was a junior at Georgia. He was director of minority recruitment and head of the newspaper on campus. "We've got to make sure we do something exciting. This will be the best time to persuade most of the students

63

to come here. I want to open up the floor for ideas of what we can do. Does anybody have any ideas?" Karlton scanned the room.

There were about fifteen people in attendance and everyone had their mouths tightly shut. I thought about many things, but I didn't want to come late and then open my big mouth. When no one said anything I slowly raised my hand.

Karlton acknowledged me. "Guys, I want to introduce you to Payton Skky. She's a freshman here and she's a very bright and lovely student from Augusta, Georgia. I asked her to join us because I felt her energy would improve our committee a great deal."

"Welcome," "Hey," and "What's up" came from different people around me.

I smiled and waved back. "Hey, I don't know if I have a lot to offer, but I definitely have some ideas. I decided to come to Georgia when I came to a recruiting visit here last year. A lot of the things you did, I would definitely say repeat. Last year when I came, it was during the fall and we got to go to a free football game, so maybe now it should be a basketball game."

"Yeah, that's a great idea," a guy replied.

"The one thing I thought was missing was maybe a Greek step show. Maybe that could be at the mixer so people can watch the show and then talk and dance and stuff."

"That would be cool," someone replied.

"Anything else, Payton?" Karlton asked.

"Well, I think we should come up with a theme and then send information to the recruits in the mail to get them hyped up about it. Everything we do should touch on the theme. That's all," I said as I quickly sat down.

"That's good stuff," he replied. "Anyone else?"

Different people started to piggyback off my ideas. I was really excited that they liked them. Before the meeting ended the committee came up with the theme "Building on History."

Since it was Black History Month we wanted to let the black students know that by coming to Georgia they could still maintain a part of who they are. I was excited about the two new organizations I had joined.

Before I could leave, Karlton offered to walk me to my car. Based on what Dakari and Rain had told me about safety, I quickly took him up on his offer.

"I'm glad you made it," he said.

"I must have gotten the time wrong."

"I didn't think you were going to show up."

"I told you I would be here when you called me last week."

"I'm glad you came. You got us going in the right direction."

"I appreciate that," I told him honestly.

"There was something I wanted to talk to you about," Karlton said.

"What?"

"I need a freshman writer for the newspaper. You interested?"

"Keep talkin'," I told him. "Why do you think I would be good?"

"You like to journal and you do good papers. Though you are a business major you said you wanted to be a sports broadcaster. I don't believe all that stuff just comes together in the end. You gotta work for it. That's what college is all about. I see potential in you and I wanna get that out. What can I say?"

"Well, how can I turn you down?"

"Don't."

"I won't."

Before I got into my car he told me a few things about the position and told me to come by the journalism office next week. Karlton told me he was very excited I was going to try out his offer. I told him I couldn't make him any promises, but I let him know that I appreciated that he believed in me enough to ask me about the job.

"We don't help one another enough," Karlton commented. "We need to make sure we're there for other people. I want my life to count for more than doing things for myself. I want to help people achieve their goals."

"I did that last year. I helped my brother's girlfriend prepare for cheerleading tryouts and she made it."

"Now that's what I'm talkin' about. God put us here for more than ourselves. He said what we do to the least we do to Him."

"I didn't know you where a religious brother."

"Yep. I've known you for six months and if you didn't know that then I'm not doin' my job."

"What do you mean?"

"I'm not talking about the Lord enough. Everywhere I go He should be on my lips and on my tongue. There are too many unsaved folks out there for me to remain silent. We can't see our future, but we can look to our past and tell folks about our experiences. The same miracles He performed in the Bible He is performing now."

"I'm sure all the college kids would love to hear how He turned water into wine," I joked.

"Naw, but when one day they don't have any money for food and the next day they are eating, that's a blessing. They can relate to that. God is truly awesome."

"I hear ya," I told him.

Karlton was a brother who had it goin' on. Not because he was cute or smart but because Christ was the center of his life. I didn't know that at first. We dated once, but I was too far into Tad and Dakari to check him out. Having him as a friend was going to be truly good for me.

We said our good-byes, he shut my car door, and I headed back to the dorm.

"Thanks, Lord," I said as I walked inside. "Thanks for

helping me see my purpose at Georgia. You've educated me in more ways than one. May I continue to be open to whatever it is that You want me to see. I love You and I thank You. In Jesus' name. Amen."

"Payton! What do we have to wear?" Robyn yelled from across the bathroom.

We were getting ready for our first recruiting visit. It seemed weird. It was only a year ago that I was a recruit. Now it was my turn to recruit someone else.

"Did you hear me, Payton? What are we wearin'?"

"Not the uniform, Robyn. Just a sweatshirt and some jeans. Weren't you listening at the meeting?"

"What do I need to listen for? You were there. I knew you were going to know."

"Girl, you are so wrong!"

We could yell because Laurel and Jewels were at their sorority meeting. We had the music blasting. It was a totally black vibe going on when they weren't around, and Robyn and I were loving it. It was cool to be us sometimes.

"Let me in, y'all!" Cammie yelled as she banged on the door.

I danced my way over to the knob and turned it.

"Look at you guys. Y'all are supposed to be ready and y'all are partyin'."

"I'm ready. I'm waitin' on Robyn."

"OK, here I come. Here I come," she said, dashing through the bathroom with her pants undone, lipstick crooked, and hair mangled.

"We got a second," I said to her, seeing she obviously needed more time.

"No, we can't be late," Cammie said. "Don't we still have to pick up Shanay and Blake? You know it takes them forever to get ready."

"OK, Cammie, call them. Robyn, you finish getting dressed and I'll pull the car around."

After all of that, when we got to Shanay and Blake's, they still weren't ready. We were late for our first official Georgia Girls function. A girl I didn't see at the first meeting was standing at the door of the athletic facility, tapping her foot and looking at her watch. She looked very familiar and she stared at me as if I did too.

"Where have you ladies been?" she said. "Georgia Girls are not on CP time. I'm the president of this organization and I don't tolerate the black chicks doing less than their job. You know what I'm saying, home girls?"

"Girl, we don't know you," Shanay told her, saying what I was thinking.

It was Shari Rice, the head hostess who was all over Dakari. From what Hayli said she was all over Drake too. Shari was now the president. If I would have known that, I wouldn't have signed up.

"Well, go on in. The football players are waiting for the recruits to show up. There is a sign for each Georgia Girl, with her football player, and her assigned recruit. Most of the football players are the freshmen and sophomore guys, so don't think you're gonna get hooked up with a big-time football player."

"What in the world is she talkin' about?" Robyn whispered in my ear.

"She's crazy. I'll tell you later," I told her.

"C'mon. Let's go see who we got," Robyn said as she tugged on my arm.

A smile came over me when I confirmed that Tad and I were going to be paired up. Our recruit was from South Carolina.

"Look at you! You got Tad! Who am I paired up with?" Robyn went to look on the list.

I scanned the room for Mr. Taylor. My eyes stopped roaming when I saw him in a heated debate with Vonda. I could almost read their lips.

"Why do you have to be paired up with her? Can't we just switch?"

"No, we don't have to go through all that trouble. It'll be cool. Payton and I are just friends."

"Dakari? What kind of name is that?" Robyn said, interrupting my thoughts.

"You're with Dakari?" I questioned.

"That's what it says. Do you know him?"

"Of course she knows me," he said, coming between us. "Dakari Ross Graham. Hey, beautiful lady," he said to Robyn.

"My name is Robyn Williams. Please use it."

"Dang. You're on the attack."

"No, I just like my name to be used."

"Well, c'mon. Let's get to know each other, Miss Robyn," he said, pulling her away.

"'Bye, Payton," she said, leaving me with a smile on her face.

I didn't even get to tell her that Dakari was my ex-boyfriend. If she knew that I'm sure she wouldn't get feelings for him and that's the way I liked it. When you want lemonade sometimes life just keeps on dealing out lemons. You've got to find water and sugar to make it all good.

I kept eyeing Tad and though he was talking to Vonda he was looking for someone. Since the recruits weren't there he had to be looking for me, but I wasn't about to get into all that. When Vonda walked away I would make sure he found me quickly. Pretty shortly, however, the recruits arrived and she hadn't walked away.

This is going to be interesting, I said to myself.

I walked up to the two of them and said, "Hey, I'm sorry to interrupt, but the recruits are here. Are you ready to go, Tad?"

Vonda didn't even speak. She gave him a look that was anything but happy. It was so awkward I didn't know what to do next.

Thankfully Tad stepped in and said, "Hey, we'll talk about this later. Right now I've got to go to work."

He walked away from both of us and went over to where the recruits were standing. He looked back at me to tell me to come on.

I walked as slowly as I could. Though I couldn't see behind me, I could feel Vonda staring at me. There was a part of the equation that I was missing. She had the guy. She had no reason to trip. If only she knew how jealous I was of her.

"Rocky Hill, this is Payton Skky," Tad said. "She will be with us tonight."

"Rocky? Is that your real name?" I asked while extending my hand.

I could tell by his gold tooth, sagging pants, and the pick stuck in the back of his head that he thought he had it going on way more than he did. The dark-skinned brother with dreads made me chuckle inside.

"Randy is my real name, but I'm a fullback and if someone gets behind me, I'm like a rock. I can't be moved. You know what I'm sayin', Miss Payton?" He took my hand and kissed it.

I quickly pulled my hand back, looked at Tad, and said, "So what's the plan? What are we doing?"

"Well, it's seven now and we have to get this guy back by eleven. It's all fun tonight. Rocky, what do you want to do?"

"Dang, you gotta excuse me, Miss Payton. I didn't know chicks at Georgia had it goin' on like this."

If that was a compliment I must have missed it. He then started walking all up on me.

Tad stepped between us and pushed him back a little bit. "Yeah, the girls at Georgia are tight, but that's not the only reason you want to come here."

"Who said I wanted to come here?" Rocky called him out.

"Dang, looks like I got my work cut out for me."

"Yeah, you do if you tryin' to get me to come here. I'm the top fullback in South Carolina."

"This year," Tad confirmed. "High school is one thing, but college is on a whole other level. Attitude is one of the first things to get checked at the door."

We piled into Tad's car. I had forgotten about my friends, but then I thought about Robyn being with Dakari. Though it wasn't a date, it bothered me slightly.

I prayed silently as I strapped myself in. *Lord, bless all of my friends tonight. We are doing something different. We put ourselves in the hands of Georgia's athletic department. Bless us all and watch over Dakari and Robyn. You know what I'm thinking before I even say it. Thanks for hearing my prayer. Amen.*

We didn't have much time. When we got to the mall it was 7:30, an hour and a half before closing. It didn't have much to offer, but Rocky wanted to see what Athens was all about.

We were sitting in the food court when Rocky started bombarding us with questions. "Do y'all really like it up here at this white school?"

"It's cool," I replied.

"The football program is outstanding. Where are you thinking about going?" Tad asked.

"South Carolina State."

"Why there?" I asked.

"Their football program is good too. And they have some players that go pro. They got all the honeys there too."

"OK," I said, "looks like you're choosing college for the wrong reasons. You said nothing about education."

"Education? I'm a ballplayer."

"What if that doesn't work out?" Tad cut in, helping me out.

"It's gonna work out 'cause I believe in my skills. Tad, you know you don't want me to go with you anyway. You know I'm gonna take your spot."

"Well, whether you come here or not, I'm gonna be number one, if the Lord allows. Plus, you're a fullback; if anything, you'll be blocking for me."

"Oh, you one of those religious brothers. God? Please, you better do it yourself."

Where in the world did this kid come from?

"Oh, wait, y'all," Rocky said. "There's a record store and there's this new rap CD I have been dying to get. Hold up."

Tad and I were left alone. We stared at each other, and in our deep gaze we were communicating on a whole different level.

My eyes were saying, *Dang, boy, you look good.*

My body language was saying, *Though I am standing five feet from you, I wish I was in your arms.*

My heart said, *Why aren't you mine?*

Tad broke the silence as he came toward me. "Rocky's a little crazy brother, ain't he?"

"Yeah, he definitely has a lot of energy. Tad, you've been quiet tonight. I noticed some tension between you and Vonda. Is everything cool?"

"Yeah, it's straight. There he is," Tad said, turning his attention back to Rocky.

Next we headed to the bowling alley. I beat both of them and we were having fun. It was almost eleven so Tad and I took Rocky back to the hotel.

Rocky grabbed my hand and tried to pull me up to his hotel room with him.

"What are you doin'?"

"I know what Georgia Girls are for. C'mon, don't you wanna help me make up my mind that I'm coming to Georgia?"

"Boy, are you stupid? Get off me."

"C'mon," he said, getting a little rougher.

All of a sudden Tad jacked him up against the wall.

"I'm gonna tell you this one time, Rocky. Payton's job is done for tonight. If you don't want to come to Georgia then that's on you, but don't you ever touch this girl or any other Georgia Girl and expect them to get with your crazy self. I don't know what you heard about the old system, but the new coach don't play that."

"It's cool, man. It's cool."

Tad let him down and Rocky came over to me. "I'm sorry. I apologize."

"Rocky, how dare you think so little of me? I'm concerned about your soul. You didn't have to play me like that."

"I'm sorry. You're fine. I just wanted to—"

"Save it," Tad told him.

"All right, Tad, man. Don't hold it against me."

Tad opened the car door and helped me inside. "Are you all right?" he asked as we drove back to the football complex.

"Yeah. I appreciate you for handling it though. I didn't send him any signals or anything. If anything, I was looking at you like that."

"What did you say?"

"Nothing."

I didn't know if he heard me or not, but I definitely meant it. He was my knight in shining armor once again.

"Hey, Burger King is still open. Do you want anything?"

I wasn't hungry, but I didn't want this night to end, so I said, "Sure, I'll get a milk shake."

We went in the drive-thru, which took thirty minutes. Though we were spending more time alone than we thought we would, we weren't really talking about much of anything. He asked me how I was doing since my grandfather passed. I told him I was doing better although I missed him a lot.

We also talked about the newfound strength I had found in my walk with Christ. I told Tad how I felt God leading me. I wanted to tell everyone about Jesus.

After he got his Whopper meal and I got my strawberry shake, he innocently grabbed my hand and said, "I wanna pray with you that all these things you're feeling about Christ continue. This is so good to hear, Payton. You are growing."

"I'd love to pray."

"Heavenly Father, we thank You for revealing Yourself to us and speaking to us in a way that we can clearly understand. Father, You know that I have been praying to You for Payton to have a walk with You that is so personal and perfect that You fill her with joy. She now has a love for You that supersedes earthly enjoyment. I pray that You continue working in her life. I also pray for Rocky. Help him to understand that football is not eternal salvation. Thank You for all You do. In Jesus' name we do pray."

"Amen," I said.

Time had gotten away from us. I had forgotten my friends were waiting for me. When we pulled into the school parking lot it was like a party outside. Everyone was having a great time. Everyone except Vonda. She had her hands on her hips.

"What's up with this? Did you forget about me or something? Where have you been?"

"Calm down. We just went to get something to eat."

"I thought *we* were getting something to eat."

She sounded so naggy it was getting on my nerves.

"Thanks," I told him.

I could tell he wanted to say more than good-bye to me, but Vonda wouldn't let him focus on anything but her.

"Why didn't you tell me your grandfather passed?" Dakari said. "I would've wanted to be there."

74

"I think your mom knew."

"I can't believe she didn't tell me."

"She probably did, but you weren't paying attention."

"Are you all right?"

"Yeah. Are y'all ready to go?" I yelled to my friends.

"Now she's trying to hurry us after being late with Tad," Shanay joked.

"For real," Blake seconded.

"I'm ready to go," Cammie said, clearly tired of the whole scene.

"Figures," Shanay said. "You've been poutin' the whole time. You better make some friends and stop actin' so anti-social."

"Where's Robyn?" I asked.

"She went to the bathroom. She'll be out in a minute." Cammie walked with me to my car and we waited.

"What's wrong with you? Why aren't you having fun like everyone else?"

"I don't know, Payton," Cammie said in an irritated voice. "They don't want to talk to me like they talk to y'all. Then you had me waitin' for forty-five minutes. That was quite selfish."

"I wasn't tryin' to be selfish. We were talkin' about the Lord and—"

"Payton, please. It's eleven-thirty on a Friday night. I'm sure the Lord was the last thing you were talkin' about in that brother's car."

"Cammie, what are you trying to say?"

"You know what I'm trying to say."

Robyn opened the car door, smiling. "Payton, you know you wrong. You didn't tell me Dakari was your ex."

"I wasn't tryin' to keep it a secret. Did he behave?"

"Did you and Tad?" Robyn asked.

"No," Cammie replied, even though no one was talking to her.

"Yes," I said.

"What is it, yes or no? Did you tell Cammie something you're not telling me?" Robyn asked.

"No, nothing happened."

By that time Blake and Shanay were back in the car.

"Girl, what's up with you and Tad? Vonda was ticked," Shanay said. "Y'all didn't want to play pool with all of us, huh?"

"We went bowling."

"Where have y'all been since eleven?"

"Looks like they were recapping the past," Robyn joked.

"He has a girlfriend," I said. "I wouldn't do that to her."

"If the man comes to you, he's yours."

"Shanay, that's why you and I had it out last semester over Dakari."

"What? What did I miss?" Robyn asked.

"Robyn, don't get too close with her ex," Shanay said.

"I'm over Dakari now."

"Yeah, because you're thinking about Tad," Blake joked.

The girlfriend talk was kind of fun. I hated that Cammie was still pouting. My friends kept teasing me about Tad. Tad and I were starting a new relationship built on Christ. We were building on history.

6

Choosing
Him Finally

I listened to my friends tease me about my relationship with Tad. I was trying to deny my feelings for him. They laughed because they knew something was going on. Deep down I had to admit it to myself. However, feeling that way was starting to bother me a lot.

"Y'all get out of the car," I joked as I dropped Blake and Shanay off.

"Don't get mad at us because you like that boy."

"'Bye," I told them in a coy voice, hoping they would get out of the car.

"Let's have breakfast in the morning," Blake suggested.

"I can't," Robyn said. "Dakari and I are taking our recruit to breakfast."

"Well, I don't have to see mine until lunch," Shanay said.

"I don't have to get together with mine until dinner," Blake added. "Payton, what about you?"

"Actually, Tad and I didn't talk about it."

Shanay commented, "Yeah, y'all were too busy talkin' about other things, or maybe y'all weren't talkin' at all."

"OK, give it a rest. My recruit was a little fresh, so I hope Tad can handle it on his own," I told them.

Cammie was quiet. She wasn't offering anything to the conversation. I knew it was time that I stopped overlooking her quietness and address it.

"Well, looks like we all have conflicting schedules," I said. "Maybe on Sunday we can hook up and go to church."

"Yeah, that sounds good. Good night," Blake and Shanay said as they got out of the car.

Robyn and I waved good-bye to them while Cammie continued to sit there. It took another two minutes for me to get to our dorm and park. I told Robyn I would see her later. I needed to talk to Cammie.

Before I could open my mouth Cammie said, "Don't even try and act like you care, Payton."

"Why are you acting like this?"

"I don't know, Payton. Maybe because ever since Robyn moved here, if we ever do anything it has to include her, and frankly, I'm not feeling that."

"Well, I didn't know it bothered you, and even if it did, that can't be what bothers you now."

"You didn't care before, so stop tryin' to act all concerned now. Dang! Can't I just go to bed?"

I grabbed her hand and stopped her from walking off. "I'm here now, Cammie. If you walk away then it's on you. Tell me what set you off."

Tears started dripping from her face as she fell into my arms.

"Cammie, what happened?"

She lifted off my shoulder, wiped her face, and replied, "At the pool hall, my recruit John-John left me and Wayne. He didn't come back for about fifteen minutes, so I went to look for him. I saw him from behind and he and another recruit were eyeing some of the other Georgia Girls. The other recruit asked John-John who was his Georgia Girl and John-John said he had to get away from me because I was so fat he was getting disgusted looking at me. He said he had to look at the real honeys. I guess I'm not a real honey. I'm just plump old me."

"First of all, it doesn't matter what other people think about you. We've been through this."

"You're only saying that to spare my feelings."

"Cammie, a little high school boy's opinion of you shouldn't matter. Girl, my recruit grabbed my arm and told me to come upstairs with him. I would much rather not have been looked at than be taken advantage of."

"I hear you, but I don't think so. Being undesirable is no fun. Of course, Payton, you wouldn't know what I'm talkin' about because you don't have those problems."

"What are you talkin' about?" I said.

"There's something about you," Cammie said, "the way you carry yourself. I think you are a great person and everything."

"I sure wish Tad Taylor thought so."

"Tad? What they were saying is true. You still like him, huh? Now it's my turn to give advice, Payton. Don't be stupid. He has a girlfriend. There are plenty of other people out there that will appreciate you."

"Maybe you're right," I told her, getting uncomfortable all of a sudden. "Girl, just don't let anybody tell you you're not cute. I'll talk to you later."

"Seems like you're rushing off. What's wrong?" she asked.

"Well, it's cold out here, for one."

"You wanna come up to my room and talk?"

"Naw. I'll call you, though."

"When? When are you gonna call me?"

"Girl, quit actin' like my mama. I said I was gonna call you."

"Yeah, whatever, Payton. I didn't think you were down with being with me," she said, storming off.

I couldn't figure Cammie out. She was really trippin'. The vibes I was getting from her were really unsettling.

"What the heck was that all about?" I mumbled to myself as I opened my dorm-room door.

Laurel's bed was empty. Someone was in the shower, and since Jewels was with Laurel, I figured it was Robyn. I lay down on my bed with the intention of getting up in a few minutes to take a shower, but I dozed off.

In my sleep, I thought about the day I first met Tad at a Georgia football game. He was introduced to me by Dakari. Tad took my hand and kissed it. He was fond of me from the first time he laid eyes on me. How I wanted him back.

My ringing phone woke me from my slumber.

"Hello?" I said in a groggy voice.

"Were you asleep?"

"Tad?" I asked, unsure of the voice on the other end.

"Yeah, it's me. I'll let you go back to sleep. We can talk tomorrow."

"No, it's OK. What are you doin' callin' me? I thought you and Vonda were hittin' the streets."

"It's twelve o'clock. I'm about to be doin' what you were doin' and hit the bed. I just wanted to make sure you got in."

"Well, it's 12:40. What did you think I would be doin' besides sleepin'?"

He didn't respond, but I wanted to tell him I was thinking about him.

"All right," he said, "I'm sorry about what Rocky said to you. I just wanted to make sure you were OK, and now that I know you are, I'll talk to you later." I realized then that Tad wasn't interested in me.

Vonda was really fortunate to have such a treasure. I'd had him and didn't even know what he was worth.

"Before you hang up, I have a question. Are we supposed to get together with Rocky tomorrow?"

"Well, because I didn't like the way he talked to you, I thought I would handle it, if you don't mind."

"That's great," I told him, happy he had made that decision.

"You know, next weekend is the Valentine's Dance and we have more recruits coming in. Maybe I'll see you there. Have a good week."

"Yeah. Good night, Tad."

After holding onto the receiver for a long time, I hung it up and rolled myself out of bed. Five minutes later I was in the shower. The hot water was therapeutic. As it hit my face, tears flowed from my eyes. I missed Tad. I missed him because I loved him. I knew then that I loved him so much that I was going to let him go. That way he could be happy with the one he was with.

"Tad?" I answered incoherently into the receiver.

"Girl, what if I was your mama and heard you askin' for a boy early in the morning?"

"Rain, what time is it?"

"It's 10:30."

"Either my roommate didn't come in at all or she's already gone. Yep, I see a note. She's gone. I didn't know it was so late. She usually wakes me up."

"You better set your own alarm."

"Girl, what do you want?" I asked in a playful way.

"I want you to come and meet my guy friend."

"Your guy friend?"

"My Morehouse brother. There's a party tonight after the basketball game. It should be pretty live. You and some of your friends should ride down. Not your white friends. I'm talkin' about the black people."

"Ha, ha, ha," I said sarcastically.

"I'm just sayin' 'cause I don't think they'll like it."

"I'll ask them and hit you back. What time do I need to call you?"

"Before three so I can get the tickets early."

I knocked on the bathroom door after hanging up with Rain.

"Yes?" Jewels said.

"Is Robyn still there?"

"Are you finally up?" Robyn called back.

"Yeah."

"OK, I'll be over in a second."

Jewels opened the door and said, "Do you need to use it?"

"Yeah, thanks."

Never before had Jewels let me know when she was done. She was changing. I was diggin' her new vibe.

"So did you and Laurel have a good time last night?" I asked.

"Yeah, we got in about one. She was so tired."

"Where is she now?"

"At the library. She studies too hard."

Robyn came into my room. "So you're finally up, huh?"

"Yeah. I thought you, your recruit, and Dakari had breakfast."

"Yeah, but I was tired. I called the front office and told them to tell Dakari to go on without me."

"So what do you have planned for today?" I asked.

"Some studying. What about you?"

"My friend Rain goes to Spelman and they have a game. I was wondering if you wanted to go."

"Yeah."

"I was gonna ask Blake and Shanay."

"What about Cammie?" Robyn reminded me.

I didn't respond.

"Is there something I should know about?" Robyn teased.

I replied, "I don't think I'm gonna ask her this time."

"You know she's gonna be mad at you."

"Well . . . anyway, I'll see you later. Go ahead and study."

"OK, count me in," Robyn said as she left to go to the library.

I looked out of the window. "Lord," I said aloud, "I wanna spend my day with you."

"Payton?" Jewels said as she popped her head into my room. "Who are you talking to?"

"I'm talking to God."

"Do you really think He can hear you like that?" she asked.

"I know He can."

"How do you know?"

"Faith."

Jewels had a bewildered look on her face as she turned around to walk into her room.

"Wait," I told her. "Jewels, I remember when I didn't know God. At one time, I even thought there was no God. When I started to think about things besides my wants and desires, I realized He was blessing me. God was there for me and still is. I can't put into words how happy God makes me. But Jewels, He can make you happy too."

Her puzzled look vanished somewhat. She took in what I said and just walked away.

"I hope I helped, Father," I said as I looked up.

Though I was imagining it, I clearly heard my grandfather say, "I'm proud of you, baby. I'm sure you helped."

"There she is! Hey, Rain!" I left all of my Georgia friends and ran into the arms of the girl I grew up with.

I was excited about being there. We were going to a party and then we were spending the night at the mayor's mansion. Blake told her parents we were coming to Atlanta and they insisted that we stay.

"I want you to meet my friends," I told Rain as I introduced her to Blake, Shanay, and Robyn.

"How are y'all doin'? So y'all are the ones that have to put up with Payton, huh?"

"Yeah, we put up with her," Blake responded.

Rain then introduced us to her roommate, Tavy. We met more Spelman girls and they were cool. It was fun being in Rain's world with her friends.

"Which one is he?" I asked her.

"You see the one that just made the basket?" she whispered in my ear. "That's him."

"Yeah."

He was a cutie with lots of game.

"The only problem is, a whole lot of girls have their eyes on him."

"So?" I said, not really caring what other girls had their eyes on.

After the game, my friends wanted to talk to some of the Morehouse guys. I felt like a groupie as I joined the many women waiting on the guys. My first thought was that we all really needed to be focused on the Lord. Boy, was I growing.

"Oh, gosh," Rain said as we got closer to Jordan. "Some girl is all over him."

Just as we approached Jordan, I noticed that the girl all over him was Robyn.

"Oh, no, she didn't! You gonna bring some chick from Georgia to flirt with my Morehouse man? Dang, I got enough people from down here that want him."

"That's all right. She didn't know."

"Well, you better talk to her."

"Rob! Come here, girl!" I called to her.

"Wait!" she said, throwing up her hand. "Can't you see that I'm busy?"

Rain hit me in the side and said, "Do something."

I went up to Robyn and said, "Excuse me" to Jordan as I pulled her away.

"What are you doin'?" she asked.

"He's taken."

"Girl, don't trip. He's not married. I didn't see no ring on his finger. If he had a girlfriend with some sense, she would be up here with him because I'm not the only one that wants him."

"The reason we came is because Rain liked some boy that she wanted me to meet, and number twenty-five that you were talkin' to . . . that's him."

"Are you serious? I didn't know. She better be glad she's your girl because I was all over that. You owe me one, Payton."

The rest of the night was uneventful. Rain shared her feelings with Jordan. They connected and he introduced Robyn to some of his boys. We partied for a little while, then headed over to Blake's and crashed.

Where was the time going? A week had passed since we were in Atlanta. It was Valentine's weekend and the football team was having a big party for the recruits. My friends were insisting that before we go to the party, we get all dressed up and go to a big, fancy restaurant and spend Valentine's Day together.

Robyn peeked her head in my room and said, "Payton, you're not dressed? We're leaving in a few minutes."

"I don't want to go."

"Payton, you know you owe me from when I backed off Rain's man. You are going. Let's go celebrate our friendship, dang it! We're leaving in ten minutes. Hurry up!"

My phone rang. It was Blake.

"Are you ready?" she asked.

"I don't want to go. Can't we just go get some pizza?"

"Just go. Shanay and I are going to meet you there."

When we pulled up to the restaurant, I didn't see Blake's car.

"We could've all rode together," I said, mad because I had to come.

As soon as we got to the door Robyn said, "I forgot something in the car. Go in and give them your name."

I opened the door and went inside the beautiful restaurant. "I have a reservation for Skky, party of four."

The maitre d' said, "I have a reservation for Skky, party of two. Follow me."

We walked past all the couples into what seemed like a private room. I was confused.

The man said, "Enjoy your evening, miss." Then he shut the door behind him.

All of a sudden music came on. As the song played, the person behind all of this stepped out of darkness.

My heart melted with sheer joy as I saw Tad. I could do nothing but cry.

As the song played, Tad came up to me with a box of chocolates and narrated the song that was playing. The first words were, *"What happened to 'I'm sorry' and 'I love you'?"*

Then Tad said, "Why don't we ever say that?"

"What happened to waiting until you are married?" were the next words.

And Tad said, "I want to be in a relationship with you where sex won't be an issue."

"What happened to a boy growing up to become a man?" was next.

"I want to be a man now that I'm in college. I want to be happy, but Payton, without you I'm not smiling. I've lost my heart. I've been praying to God and He revealed to me that

I need you in my life."

"What about Vonda?" I asked as tears poured from my eyes.

"I had to be honest with her. I told her my heart belonged to another, and she told me that she knew. We're still friends."

"You did all this for me?" I asked, as I could hardly believe my eyes. "This room is beautiful. It must've cost a fortune."

"You are more than worth it," he said with a love in his eyes that I hadn't thought I would see again.

He set the box of chocolates on the table, pulled me into his arms, and we danced to the beautiful gospel song. It was like the Lord was dancing with us. I had Christ in a way that I never had Him before and now I had Tad again. Life could not be better. God had given us to each other, and I wasn't going to mess it up this time. We prayed and thanked Him for allowing us to be together.

Tad picked up a Valentine card off the table and said, "Payton Skky, will you accept my heart and be my Valentine?"

I took the gift from him, hugged him tight, and wept once again. "I'd love to be your Valentine," I said, kissing him on the cheek.

Tad and I were committed to each other for the long haul. We were gonna do it right this time. I was happy that I was choosing Him finally.

7

Meeting
Good People

*W*e were hand in hand. This was the best surprise of my life and I wanted to tell him so, but before I could, our waiter came in.

"Mr. Taylor, my name is Vincent and I'll be your server. I want to start you and your girlfriend off with some sparkling apple cider. You two make a lovely couple."

I smiled.

Throughout the meal, Vincent not only served us but gave us inspirational thoughts as well.

When he brought our dessert—cheesecake in the shape of a heart with fresh raspberries on top—he asked a question. "So now you guys are happy and back together again, but are you going to stay that way? What will hold you together?"

We believed God was the glue that would hold us together. If we did part, then it was God's will. We were both committed to being committed to our relationship. That was the response we gave to Vincent.

He smiled and replied, "I see you guys are going to make it. Y'all got it goin' on. Just make sure you treat each other the way God wants you to, and He won't let you down."

Vincent left and Tad said, "You know, he's right."

"I know. I'm so thankful that we're back together. I love praying with you. I love being with you. I love you," I told him.

"It feels right now, huh?" Tad asked.

"Most definitely."

"We're supposed to go to the football party. I don't want to go, but Rocky is back and I think the coach wants to sign him. Is it cool with you that we go?"

"Yeah. A few more minutes with you will be great."

Tad helped me from my seat, took my hand, and said, "I forgot to tell you how beautiful you look this evening."

"By giving me this night, you make me feel beautiful. I'm so happy."

"Me too."

―――――――――――――

Tad grabbed my hand and we entered a party that was jamming. This was how it was supposed to be. I no longer had to watch him from a distance and wish he was mine.

As soon as we stepped into the place, my girls grabbed me from Tad.

"She'll see you in a minute. We got to get the scoop," Robyn announced to Tad.

The four of us went to the corner and I told Blake, Shanay, and Robyn about my magical evening.

"I don't know whether to hug you guys or get you guys," I said. "Y'all know y'all were wrong for playing that trick on me."

"You made it hard for us," Robyn said.

"Yeah, talkin' about how you didn't want to get dressed up and spend no money. You should have known something was up because I wouldn't spend no money with y'all anyway," Shanay said.

"You ain't kiddin', Shanay. She should've known 'cause you are the cheapest of all of us," Blake said.

We all laughed.

"Y'all have to tell me how you did it," I requested.

Robyn explained, "Tad just asked us to help him and I was a little shocked because I thought he had a girlfriend."

Proudly I announced, "He does have a girlfriend."

"Oh, don't get cute, Payton," Shanay retorted.

"For real, though," Blake said. "Vonda's right over there. She's been to herself all night."

"I went into the bathroom," Robyn explained, "and I caught the girl cryin'."

"Oh, don't tell me that," I said, starting to feel guilty.

"She's been hangin' out with some white girl. So he broke up with her for you, huh?"

"Yeah, but he did that before he knew I would accept being with him again. Tad said even if he knew we wouldn't be together, he knew he didn't want to be with her."

Shanay and Blake went on their way after giving me hugs of congratulations.

Robyn said, "I'm really excited for you. If Jackson was half the man Tad is, I would want to get back with my ex too. Don't mess it up this time."

"I won't. Laurel is not going to believe this. Did you guys tell her?"

"No, she's always on the run. I haven't even seen her lately. I'm so happy for you." Robyn hugged me. What a true friend she was. She was still going through her heartbreak, but she helped Tad and me get back together. I was blessed in a lot of ways.

As I started making my way through the crowd to find

Tad, I ran into Coach Randolph.

"Honey, here is the young lady who told me where my wallet was," he said to his wife.

"Well, hello, I'm Cameron Randolph," she said, extending her hand.

"Hi, I'm Payton Skky."

"My husband said he knew he made the right decision to come to Georgia when one of the students was so honest and helped out a complete stranger."

"I didn't do much. I just did what I would have wanted someone to do for me," I tried explaining.

"Yeah, but when you're good at heart, you're just doing what God's Word wants you to do, you bless other people. When you allow God to use you, He blesses you even more."

It had been leaked to the media that the coach was a Christian. Having his wife give me a biblical message was inspiring. She pulled out a piece of paper and said she would love to sit down and have tea with me.

"I'd love that," I told her.

"OK, well, let's do it soon."

They walked away from me and I went looking for Tad once again.

Rocky came up to me and said, "Hey, you remember me?"

"Yeah, Rocky, I do."

"You want something to drink or anything?"

"No, thanks, I'm going to the ladies' room."

When I got into the ladies' room, there was a familiar person inside. It was Tad's ex-girlfriend. I quickly asked God to help me say the right thing.

"Vonda, are you OK?" I asked with concern.

"What do you think, Payton? Just get out of my face."

"I don't mean to be insensitive, Vonda."

She stood firmly and said, "Did you come to rub it in? He chose you over me." She stormed out of the bathroom.

I walked out and saw Tad standing at the door.

"Payton. What did you say to her?"

"I tried to fix things, but she wasn't hearin' it."

Rocky stepped in front of us. "I was tryin' to get a dance, Payton. I wanna get my groove on. C'mon," he said as he tried to grab my hand.

Tad stepped in and said, "Man, Payton is my girl. She ain't gonna be dancin' with you."

"Dang, I didn't know that was you. I'm sorry," he said as he backed away.

I waved at Rocky as Tad led me to his car.

"I am so blessed that we're together. I love you," I said to Tad.

A few minutes later we were in front of my dorm. I hugged my boyfriend and thanked him once again for the special evening.

He kissed me on the cheek and told me the evening was special to him too. We prayed for the Lord to bless us.

"So how was your evening?" Laurel asked as I came into the room.

"Oh, my roommate. I haven't seen you in so long, I forgot what you looked like," I joked.

"Ha-ha. Give me all the details," she said. "I hear you and Tad are back together."

"Yes, yes, yes," I said as I jumped on my bed. "He's my boyfriend again."

"I'm happy for you. Don't blow it, Payton, because I know how you are."

"I won't."

Things were perfect. God had given me all the desires of my heart. It was a great Valentine's night.

"So you guys finally have a running-back coach. It's almost March."

"Yeah, I know," Tad told me as we spoke on the phone two weeks later.

We had been inseparable. I was glad that I had friends who understood because I was spending most of my time away from them. They were actually happy for me. Everyone except Cammie. It was as if she'd turned into a whole different person. She left several messages on my machine and several notes on my door. It wasn't stalking, but it was way too obsessive. Since her messages were bothering me, I had been avoiding her.

I talked to Tad about Cammie and he said, "Just pray for her. Maybe she hasn't had a close friend and she is bothered by not having you around."

I told him that I could understand that, but it didn't make it any easier. However, prayer was a good solution. "So are you sure the coach wants me to go out to dinner with you guys?"

"Yeah. Coach Randolph said he wanted me to meet my new running-back coach. He asked about you and me and I told him we were tight. He wants us to go out with the running-back coach and his wife."

"Do you think he'll be boring?"

"I've never met a football coach that was boring. I think he may be a Christian. Can you be ready in a couple of hours?"

I asked, "Yeah, but what should I wear?"

"Just wear something nice."

"You mean casually cute?"

"Just look like you always do," Tad responded.

I had two hours before my big date. Laurel was in the room and we read Proverbs together. We read up through chapter three. My favorite Scripture was verses five through six, which said, "Trust in the Lord with all thine heart; and lean not unto thine own understanding. In all thy ways acknowledge him, and he shall direct thy paths."

"What are you thinking about?" Laurel asked as I stared at the wall.

"Just recalling how awesome God really is. When I got out of the way, He worked things out like they should be. I was not letting Him be Lord. Now I can truly say that He can do it and He does not need my help. How about you? How are things goin'?"

"I'm still dealing with a lot of stuff, but I'm better. I'm heading to the library to study."

"OK. Is something else at the library besides books?"

"What are you talking about, Payton?"

"You can study anywhere on this campus, and you continue to go to the library. Something is going on."

"You get dressed for your date. My night's not going to be nearly as exciting as yours."

"Well, you better have straight A's this semester."

"You study a lot, too."

"Yeah, but I do it here, on the Internet."

"I use the Internet, too. Only I use it in the nice, quiet environment of the library."

"Whatever."

"So where are we going?" I asked Tad, excited about being with him.

"We're going to meet them at Coach Randolph's house. He said he thinks I'll like the new coach."

"Hello," Coach Randolph's wife said as she opened the door. "Well, Payton, it's nice to see you again. You're Mr. Taylor, right?"

"Yes, ma'am," Tad answered.

The head coach came over and thanked us for taking the time to come to his home. Tad's mouth hung open when he saw that the new running-back coach was Darius Mullins,

Tad's high school running-back coach.

They hugged like they missed each other very much. My face lit up when almost-eight-months-pregnant Shayna, his wife, wobbled toward me. I dashed to her.

"It's so good to see you," I said. "I can't believe your husband is the new coach here."

Shayna had never gotten the chance to disciple me, but it looked like the opportunity had presented itself again. God was truly good.

"How did you get this job?" Tad asked Darius.

Darius responded, "Coach Randolph said you told him about me. He told me—"

Coach Randolph cut in, "I told him that if he can do with you what he did in high school, we could win some championships."

"Wow! Well, Coach, I think you got the right man for the job," Tad told him.

"Do you know what you're having?" I asked Shayna, looking at her belly.

"No, we didn't want to find out with our first."

Although Shayna was bigger than I had ever seen her, she was smiling from ear to ear. I was truly happy for her.

Coach Mullens and Tad rode together in Coach's van following Shayna and me as we drove to drop Tad's car back on campus.

"So tell me how you and Tad are really doing," she said as we were having our girl talk before joining the guys.

I told her all about the romantic evening Tad and I had. I still couldn't believe Tad and I were back together again. I told her God had sent her back into my life to keep me on the right track.

"Payton, I don't want you to think I don't have faults. I've been having crazy mood swings lately. I'm really happy for Darius getting this coaching position, even though this move has been really hard. I'm proud of him, but I'm not perfect."

"Yeah, but you're where I want to be."

"It looks like you're getting there. I'm excited that the Lord has allowed me to run into you. I'm definitely glad that you and Tad worked things out."

As the four of us were riding down the street in the Mullenses' new minivan, Shayna mentioned that her stomach was tightening. Before we got to the restaurant, she was in labor. Her water broke in the car.

I used my cell phone and called the hospital. I told the emergency room we were on our way. We were all relatively new to Athens, so unfortunately we got lost. Things were getting really scary. Shayna was screaming uncontrollably, Darius was panicking, I was crying because I was scared, and Tad was praying.

"Lord, help us!" he said over and over.

Pretty soon the hospital was staring us straight in the face. Even though Coach Mullens was nervous, he took care of his wife in good fashion.

Shayna asked me to come in the room with her during the birth. I was honored and humbled that she'd asked me.

"The baby shouldn't be coming now," Shayna mumbled to the doctor. "It's too early."

The doctor got the fetal monitor to check the baby. The heartbeat seemed irregular.

Tad and I waited nervously for our friends.

"There's another strong heartbeat," the doctor said. "Something is not right. Let me check again. Did your doctor tell you that you're having twins? I think I hear two different heartbeats."

"No. We've been to the doctor many times and he has never mentioned anything like that. It can't be so," Shayna said.

"Well, that would explain why your babies have come now and why you're a little larger than normal. Yes, there they are. See them on the monitor? There are two babies," the doctor explained. "However, one heartbeat is weakening and we're going to rush you in for an emergency C-section."

As Tad and I waited in the hallway, we held hands and said no words. I remembered being in the clinic with Lynzi praying that she would have no baby. Now I was praying for the healthy delivery of two.

Lord, I thought, *You have a timing and a purpose for everything. I have never met a nicer couple than the Mullenses. I just pray for Shayna and Darius . . .*

I couldn't even finish my prayer. I just dropped my hand from Tad's and placed my head in it. I was feeling Shayna's pain.

Tad stroked my hair and said, "It's going to be OK."

We waited another hour before we got word from Darius. The smile on his face said it all. Tad was right. It was OK.

"Tell us about the babies," I said, wiping my face.

"We have a little girl and a little boy," Darius told me.

"No way!" I screamed. "Is everyone OK?"

"Yeah, I'm excited. They're both very small and in incubators, but the doc said he's pretty confident they'll be OK. Shayna said she wanted to say good night to you guys and tell you thank you."

"I'd love to see her," I told him.

"OK. I'll call for you in a little while."

Tad and I stood in the hallway and hugged. It was good to share in Darius and Shayna's joy.

"Do you wanna know the names of the babies?" Shayna asked after thanking us. "Our son's name is Taylor Austin Mullens."

"Shayna's maiden name was Taylor, but she was sold on Taylor because of you, Tad," Darius explained.

"And our daughter's name is Skky."

"Are you serious?" I asked.

"Yes. I want you both to know how much you mean to me."

"Wow! I don't know what to say. This means a great deal

to me. Thanks. What's Skky's middle name?"

"Auburn, after the school where her dad went," Coach Mullens bragged.

"Oh, that's so cute!" I exclaimed.

"Well, we're gonna let y'all get some rest," Tad said as he attempted to pull me from the room.

"I'll be back tomorrow to see the little people," I told her.

"OK," Shayna said. "Please come back."

It was such a special night. On our way out Tad and I saw the nurse roll the babies to the neonatal unit. They were so tiny. It was as if they were the size of footballs. They were precious.

"Hi, Taylor. Hi, Skky," I said as the nurse rolled them by. "This is Tad and I'm Payton. It's so nice to meet you guys. We've been praying for you. We love you. I can't believe the babies are named after us. We'll have to get them something tomorrow," I told Tad. "You wanna go baby shopping with me?"

"Not for one of my own," Tad joked.

"Oh, no, you don't have to worry about that," I said as I hit him. "But aren't they cute? I'm worried about them."

"You've got to look past all that and see what God sees," Tad said. "When God looks at us, He looks past our faults and sees what He's created."

Tad and I grew closer that night. We were sharing very special things and I knew it was only going to get better.

"Is there a problem or something, Payton?" Tad asked me as we walked through the packed coliseum.

We were going to watch the men's basketball game against LSU. I hadn't gotten to see Tad all day because I was at the hospital with Shayna. This was supposed to be our fun time, but he'd invited one of his football buddies.

"I just thought it would be good for him to get out. All he does is go to the library and study. I was already gonna be here with you, so I told him to come along."

"So what are you saying? You would have went with him if you weren't going with me? Well, I can go home."

"Don't get an attitude."

He was right. I shouldn't mind sharing him. "Where's the guy?"

"He's probably already sitting down. He's pretty punctual."

"A guy being punctual?"

"It could happen."

As soon as Tad introduced me to Casey Hanson, I thought about how adorable he was. Laurel would love him. I sat between Casey and Tad and he was pretty cool. I could see why Tad liked hanging out with him.

"Payton, Casey is our kicker. He's from Washington."

"Oh, you're from D.C. My girlfriend—"

"No, I'm from Washington State."

The guys both laughed at me.

"Well, I didn't know. Do you like it in the South?"

"Yeah, people seem a lot nicer down here."

"Why did you come to the University of Georgia instead of going to Washington?"

"A lot of the schools that wanted me already had upper-classmen kickers and I wanted the opportunity to kick as a freshman."

"So you started this year?" I asked.

"Toward the end."

"Oh, yeah," Tad said, "you were the only other person who scored points for us."

Casey smiled. "Tad and I got together and found out we have other interests besides football. We have the Lord."

"Cool. So you don't have a girlfriend?"

Tad nudged me in the arm. "Don't try and hook him up."

"I really don't need to get matched up. Although it would be great to have what you guys have, right now I'm busy loving the Lord. I'm studying and training for football. I don't have much time for anything else."

"I'm sure you could make time. My roommate Laurel is really cute."

It was now halftime and the cheerleaders came out. It was the first time I had checked them out and none of them looked like me.

"Where are all the black cheerleaders?" I asked.

Casey said, "They don't have any."

Tad said, "Yeah, Pay, you should try out."

Then I saw the girls flipping from one side of the court to the other.

"I can't do that!"

"I don't know you, but you don't strike me as the type of person to give up because something is hard. You'll go get them."

Casey was nice and sweet to me. My roommate had been sad too long; she needed a sweet guy.

"Are you gonna come with us to get something to eat?" Tad asked Casey.

"No, I'm going to go and study. Payton, thanks for letting me crash in on your date."

"No," I told him. "It was fun. I'm looking forward to seeing you again. It's always nice meeting good people."

8

Sharing My Faith

So, Laurel," I said, talking to my roommate days after meeting a handsome guy named Casey Hanson, "I believe you need a boyfriend."

"What?" she said, looking totally confused and agitated.

"Oh, c'mon. You've been walking around here all gloomy."

"Payton, I have not been gloomy. Just because I've been studying day and night, you're practically calling me a nerd."

"Well, let's just imagine you met the right guy. One who's cute, a Christian, and an athlete."

"Been there, done that. It didn't work out. Remember Foster, the high school boyfriend I told you about?"

"Yeah, but Foster's all the way across the world. You need someone here."

"You know somebody like that?" she said, a little bit interested.

"Yes, I do, Laurel. Let me hook it up and get you two together."

"A blind date? No."

"No? Is that your final answer?"

"Yes, Payton. That's my final answer."

Though she said no, I was determined that that wasn't going to be the way it went down. I could give Laurel some time and pretty soon she would come around. She wanted companionship, no matter what she said.

I started thinking about myself. We had to push back the SGA event from February to March, meaning it was this weekend. I had several meetings to attend. Maybe it was a good thing Laurel didn't want to get together with Casey just yet. My plate was already full.

I thought about cheerleading. Could I possibly make the team? No, I couldn't even do those flips.

"It's OK, Payton. I'm glad you're trying to make me happy, but I'm not interested," Laurel said.

"I'm not even thinking about that."

"Really? Well, you seem to be in very deep thought. What are you thinking about?"

"I'm thinking about trying out for cheerleader, but I can't do those flips," I told her.

"Really? I was thinking about trying out too. I can do the flips and jumps but not the dances, and I can't remember the cheers."

We began brainstorming and talking to each other about our strengths and weaknesses. It sounded as if wherever she was strong, I was weak and wherever I was strong, she was weak. It was cool because we made an agreement to help each other.

I stood up right then and taught her a cheer. It took us a while, but she finally got it. She then told me to put on my sweats because we were heading to the gym.

When we got there, I was distraught because I couldn't even begin to get those flips. Then Laurel got discouraged because she had a hard time doing the cheers. So we held hands and prayed. We encouraged each other, lifted up our burdens to the Lord, and vowed to give our tryouts all we had.

"We'll get it," Laurel said as we headed back to the dorm.

"I hope so."

"So why did you choose to come here, Payton?" a girl named Cree asked me candidly.

Recruiting weekend for minority students was finally here. I was running around frantically trying to make sure things were in order, and that wasn't even my job. It was Karlton's, but he commented to me earlier how thankful and blessed he was that I was on board. I couldn't possibly let him down now.

Before I could finish making sure things were in order, Cree stopped me and told me she was seriously considering coming to UGA. She wasn't 100 percent sure of her choice, but she was close.

"Cree, that's a pretty name," I said. "Where are you from?"

"Marietta, Georgia."

"Well, coming to UGA won't be that far from home."

"I know," she responded. "That's why I'm thinking it won't be the best choice. Why did you come here?"

"To be honest, I don't think my reasons were the right ones."

"What do you mean?"

"I had two ex-boyfriends who were coming to this school. If you have any guy friends here, I would not recommend UGA as your first choice. I have some friends who have done so and regretted it."

"That's not the case for me, but I'm still not sure if I want to be here."

"What's the problem?"

103

"I went to a predominantly white high school and I'm not sure if I want to go to a predominantly white college. I want to have experience being in a black world. Does that make any sense?"

"Yeah, a lot. That's the main reason I decided to come to Georgia. My first high school was black, and I wanted to see what the real world was like before I got up in it as an adult. Maybe you should try a black school if that's what you want."

"So you're a part of the committee for minority recruitment and you're suggesting that I don't go here?"

"No. I'm saying your reasons for not wanting to attend UGA are valid, and those are worth considering before choosing a school. You also have to take into consideration where your parents may want you to go."

"Georgia gave me a scholarship, so my parents want me to come here."

"You should also look at extracurricular activities. Maybe you can study and have fun."

"You've given me a lot to think about. Thanks for sharing. Your thoughts have shed a lot of light for me."

"Oh, really? That's good. I thought I'd confused you."

"No, you didn't."

"Well, let me know what you decide. Georgia would be a lot better if you decided to come here."

"That's very nice of you to say," Cree said as she hugged me.

"Can I cut in there and get one?" the voice of my ex said.

"Well, speak of the devil," I blurted aloud. "Who do you want a hug from, Dakari? Me or Cree?"

"Cree? Is that this pretty lady's name?"

"Yeah, hi," she said, batting her eyes at Dakari.

I could tell if she went to a historically black college she was going to get into some serious trouble. She was trying to get with the first cute boy she saw. I was going to have to keep an eye on her because she was too sweet to get caught up in the trying-to-find-a-man syndrome.

"Excuse me, Cree," Dakari said. "I just need to steal this lady from you for one second."

"That's OK," Cree said. "We're done. Thanks, Payton. It was nice talking to you. What's your name again?"

"Oh, my bad. I'm Dakari Graham."

"Maybe I will have to go here, Payton," she said on the sly before she walked off.

I pulled Dakari to the side and said, "See what you're doin'? You've corrupted the little high school girl's mind."

"If I could only get the girls that go here to think the same, I would have it goin' on," he said as he started grabbing at my waist and pulling me close to him.

"Don't even start, Dakari," I said, pulling away.

"For real, let me talk to you."

"What?" I said. I smelled alcohol on his breath. "Ugh, boy, get back. You've been drinking!"

"Oh, Payton. Don't play me like that."

We went over to the corner and every time I stepped back, he took two steps forward.

"What do you want?" I asked.

"I heard you and my roommate Tad were goin' together. Tell me that ain't true, Payton," he said with droopy eyes. "I thought you wanted a real man."

I had no idea where this conversation was going, but Dakari had become the guy I despised. He kept coming toward me until my head was pushed against the wall and his hands were on either side of me.

"What is this, Dakari? Get back!"

"Payton, if you're goin' to be with that brotha, the least I could get is a good-bye kiss."

"A what? Negro, you better get out of my face. You're talkin' crazy."

"No, you're actin' crazy. All I want is a kiss. Now c'mon!"

"Why can't you accept the fact that I've chosen someone else?"

"Payton, you don't know who you really want. Just let me kiss you so I can show you what's up. I know you, and Tad ain't been up to nothin'. We in college now. Ain't no one still doin' that elementary holdin' hands stuff."

Dakari quickly kissed me on the lips. He was more than twice my size, and pushing him back was not working. From the corner of my eye I spied Tad. What in the world was I going to do? Tad just walked by as I finally managed to push Dakari away.

"Tad!"

"You wanna go after him?" Dakari said loudly, causing a scene. "Forget you then, girl! Yo' punk behind better keep walkin'!"

"Tad, wait!"

Dakari pulled my arm and kept me from going after Tad. I guess he wanted me to stay after all.

"Let go!"

"Why are you so upset, baby? That just proves you don't need him."

"I didn't want you to kiss me, and even if I had let you, it would have been a good-bye kiss. Good-bye means it's over."

Tad was way on the other side of the room. He never looked back on my struggle with Dakari. However, there was a crowd around Dakari and me. Dakari was really looking stupid and making me look stupid as well.

"Dakari, man, let her go!" someone yelled from the crowd.

At that point I was crying. I hated seeing Dakari in that state. I also hated what he had done to me and Tad.

"Man, you better get up off me!" Dakari yelled to Karlton as he tried to help me get loose.

Dakari started swinging at Karlton. When he let me go, I ran to the person yelling, "Come here, Payton!"

I buried my head in Hayli's chest. "What are you doing here?" I asked.

"I came up here with Drake because I had to help Karlton."

"You didn't tell me you were coming."

"I didn't know until recently. Drake just came to show out."

"He can't be doing any more than his brother."

"Look, man," Karlton told Dakari, "I'm going to have to ask you to leave if you don't calm down."

Dakari was giving Karlton a hard time, and Karlton turned to call security. Dakari raised his hand to hit Karlton. On instinct I ran to push Karlton out of the way and got socked in the eye. When I fell to the ground, it must have damaged my nose because I started bleeding.

"Payton, I'm sorry," Dakari said with slight emotion.

"Get off me! Get off me!" I screamed.

Drake found his way to the circle with two girls on each side of him. He had his arm around their waists and red lip prints were all over his face. Hayli looked devastated, yet she tended to me.

"I can't believe this. I can't believe he would embarrass me like this," I moaned, holding my eye.

The next few minutes were hazy because all I remember was Tad and Karlton helping me out of the facility. Dakari and Drake were nowhere to be found.

"I didn't want to be with him. He kissed me, Tad. I didn't want to kiss him. You've got to believe me."

"I know, babe. It's cool. I should have known Dakari was bothering you. He and his brother came into the room and they were both talking stupid. I could tell they had been drinking."

"You know I didn't want to be around him," I told Tad.

"I saw you getting away from him so I thought that was the end of it. We almost got to fighting earlier tonight and I didn't want to get into anything else. Now you got hurt and it's all my fault," Tad said as he placed me in the back of his car.

"No, it's not," I told him as he started the engine. "It's not your fault."

"It's not your fault, either, Payton."

"Where are we going?" I asked.

"To the infirmary."

"I'm OK, Tad."

"Your eye is black-and-blue, Payton. I don't want your nosebleed to start back up. You at least need to get checked out."

"I don't want to."

"I'm not gonna hear anything else about it. I won't be OK until I know you're OK. I'll have to deal with Dakari later."

Our relationship had been drama-free for the last two weeks. Thanks to Dakari, the roller-coaster ride was back open for business. I hated seeing Tad frustrated. Though the scene with Dakari was bad, I was definitely glad to see that it was over.

———————

Well, I thought it was over. I was lying in the infirmary with the screen closed when the police officer and the doctor came back in to question me.

"Did the gentleman who brought you in here do this to you?" the officer asked.

"Huh?" I said, out of it.

"You don't have to worry, you'll be protected. Did Tad Taylor do this to you?"

"No, officer. No," I said with a small voice.

"We see this kind of stuff all the time. We know he's your boyfriend and you want to protect him, but it doesn't

108

matter. I'm tired of these athletes getting away with murder."

"It was an accident."

"Oh, so you're saying he did do it?"

"No, he didn't do this! Tad!" I yelled.

He came rushing in. "I told you I didn't do it. Payton just got caught in the crossfire."

"Crossfire of what?" the officer asked.

"These two other guys were fighting," I told them.

"That just doesn't sound logical," the doctor put in.

We stayed there another twenty minutes and had to go over the whole story again. The officer finally decided not to press charges against Tad.

I fled to Tad's arms when they released me from the room.

"Look at her running to him," the cop said, disgusted.

"It's so unfair of them accusing you like this," I told Tad.

"Just let it go, Payton."

"No, I won't. I don't know why they can't take my word for it," I said, frustrated. "Do you think he would have brought me here if he did this?" I asked the officer.

"We've seen stranger things than this," the officer commented. "Your situation is nothing new or special. Some girls don't love themselves enough to protect themselves. Ma'am, if you want to be in that category when something else happens, at least we can say that we tried."

"Well," I told him, "you can't say just because things look a certain way, that's the way they are. Every case is different. This guy right here is the sweetest man I know. He actually walked away from the fight. He prays and asks the Lord to work things out."

"Ma'am, that's all fine and good, but what does that have to do with anything?"

"I'm saying that you have to look at things on a case-by-case basis."

"That's why we are letting him go."

"Do you know the Lord?" I asked the tough officer.

"My sister was a Christian and her husband killed her. I wonder where her God was then."

Tad stepped in and said, "I'm sorry about what happened to your sister, but sometimes bad things happen to good people."

"Is that supposed to be some kind of consolation to me? My sister is dead!"

"I'm not saying He wanted her dead. Her life should not have ended like that, but she is in a much better place now."

"So that's how you guys do it, huh? You beaters think the lady is better off dead, right?" the cop said, losing his temper.

"I pray that you'll understand," Tad told him as we left.

Tad was so mad he couldn't even look at me. There was no way we could have known that our trip to the infirmary would end up this badly.

"At least we told the guy about God," I told him.

"Yeah, but I can't believe he accused me of hitting you. I love you. I would never hit you."

When we got in the car, I asked, "Is witnessing always that hard?"

"Witnessing is hard, but every time you plant the seed, the Lord comes along and nurtures it. Our job is to let people know who is the King of kings. How are you feeling?"

"I'm OK. Are you sure you're OK?" I asked Tad as I noticed his sad eyes.

When he didn't answer my question, I prayed aloud, "Lord, the night has been very eventful and not in a good way. Tad and I are stressed to the max. May we both stay encouraged in telling the world who You are. We love You, Lord, and we know You love us. Thanks for sticking with us through the tough times. Give us Your strength."

"Thanks, baby," he said, putting his arm around me. "I needed that. Let me get you home. This day has been long enough."

"I know. I don't think I can handle anything else. I'm wiped out," I confessed, "but at least I can say the tough stuff isn't so bad when I go through it with you."

"Well, it's over now," he said as he stroked my hair. I closed my eyes and almost went to sleep.

Before we got to my dorm, my cell phone rang. As soon as I answered it, screams screeched in my ear. "Oh my God, Payton! You've got to come! He's got a gun!"

"Come where? Who has a gun? Robyn, what's going on?"

"A gun?" Tad repeated, totally freaked out.

"Robyn, what's going on?"

"We're at Club Jade and he started shooting."

"Club Jade!" I repeated to Tad.

Tad turned the car around and headed toward the club we knew to be trouble.

"Robyn, are you all right?"

"It's Dakari, Drake, and some other guys who used to play football at UGA."

"What's going on?"

"There was an argument and a fight broke out. One of the local guys pulled a gun on the football players. Oh my God!"

I heard the gunshots as if I were there.

"Robyn, who was shot? Are they OK?"

"I've got to go," Robyn said, sobbing, before she hung up on me.

"I don't know why they would go to Club Jade," Tad said. "You know, someone was stabbed there last semester."

"Oh my God! Someone's hurt," I said as we got to the scene moments later and I saw an ambulance driving away. "I hope it's not Dakari."

I realized after I said that that I shouldn't have. I might have hurt Tad's feelings.

However, my guy surprised me when he said, "I pray it's not Dakari too."

It looked like a massacre. I heard a familiar voice moan. Dakari was embracing someone.

Robyn must have spotted me because she ran up and said, "Payton, it was horrible," as she hugged me tight.

Tad went to console Dakari.

Robyn explained to me that Dakari's older brother, Drake, took two shots to his chest. Drake and Dakari and the other football players were talking about Drake's signing bonus from the Atlanta Falcons when some local guys declared that Drake wasn't worth his money. Dakari and Drake tried to leave, but shots were fired. One of the players shot back and hit the two locals, but they were only wounded.

"Oh my gosh!" I could only hug her because I was glad that she and Shanay were OK.

I looked at Tad and Dakari. Dakari was still rocking back and forth, holding Drake.

"Sir, we need to take him away. Your brother has been killed," the paramedic said to Dakari in a caring tone.

"No! Leave my brother alone! He's OK!"

"C'mon, Dakari," Tad said, trying to ease the situation.

"Leave me alone, man! Get back!" Dakari yelled to Tad.

"We need to take him," the paramedic said again.

Dakari still wasn't letting go. "This can't be happening. You've got it all, Drake. Can't no bullet stop you. C'mon, man," he said, sobbing.

Tad pulled Dakari up as the rescue workers took Drake. Dakari fell into Tad's arms and they shared a moment that I'm sure changed the course of their relationship. In the hour of sadness for Dakari, he was not alone. We were all by his side.

As the ambulance pulled away, Dakari noticed me and said, "Call my parents, Payton."

The police officer came up to me, "Do you know the

number of the young man's parents?"

"Yes, sir."

"Can you dial them up?"

It was 1:30 in the morning, and I didn't want to make that call. To my surprise the officer gave Dakari's parents the horrific news. Then he handed the phone to Dakari as he cried once again.

After he hung up the phone, the police took Dakari down to the station to press charges against the shooters.

I went up to Dakari and said, "God's got this."

"Girl, get out of my face with that mess! My brother is dead! Where was God an hour ago! I'm not tryin' to hear it!"

"It's cool," Tad whispered in my ear. "I'm going to stay with Dakari. Are you going to be OK?"

"Yeah, Robyn can give me a ride home."

"All right, be careful."

It was the most horrible night of my life. All I knew to do was talk about Jesus. Dakari wasn't the only one who didn't understand why this had to happen. In the coming days and weeks, he and his family were going to need the Lord. Even though he rejected me at that moment, I was glad I was sharing my faith.

9

Caring
for Friends

*T*his is heartbreaking," my mom told me as she held my
hand at Drake's funeral back in Augusta.

I hadn't gone to many funerals, but this was definitely
the saddest one I had been to in my entire life. Blake,
Shanay, and Robyn rode down with me and spent the night
at my house. We all stayed up really late talking about how
horrible this was. When you know Christ, death isn't a bad
thing. However, when the soul doesn't know the Lord, it is
terrible. Drake was dead. The end. Eternal damnation. Eternal separation from Christ.

Dakari's mom was sobbing uncontrollably. Hayli was as
stiff as a board. Dakari had shown me lots of emotion, but I
had never seen him this upset. Pieces of my heart were
damaged as I watched him go through his pain. Dakari lost
it. He went up and hugged his brother, grabbed his neck,
and tried to pull him from the casket. His mom couldn't
take it and almost passed out while his dad tried to calm
Dakari down.

The media was covering the funeral because Drake was an Atlanta Falcon, and a lot of his teammates and coaches were there. I guess it should have made it more comforting that he was so important, but it didn't. Drake led a great life, but what good would that do him in hell? The pastor who knew him was tiptoeing around the issue. He was trying to say great things about Drake's life, but it didn't matter because he wasn't going to heaven.

The Scripture, "What shall it profit a man, if he shall gain the whole world, and lose his own soul?" had great meaning to me now. Drake had it all and now he was going to leave it all here. The preacher did a great job doing the eulogy on the importance of knowing God. He stated that it was the biggest touchdown you could score.

Throughout the service, Dakari never had total composure. But as Drake's body was wheeled out of the church and his mom went hysterical, Dakari took a manly stance and stayed strong for his mother.

I rode in the car with my parents, and my friends drove my car behind us.

"Mom, it was so sad, so different from Granddaddy's funeral. It seemed so final."

"If what they say is true," my dad replied with passion and honesty, "and Drake hadn't accepted the Lord, then today is a very sad day. It makes me know that I need to do more in my life than sell cars. Everyone that walks in that dealership needs to know about the Lord."

I sat in the back and tears flowed because I realized that maybe I hadn't done my part with Drake.

"Don't you go blaming yourself, Payton," my mom said to me. "I've known Drake ever since he was young and he stopped coming to church so that he could watch football on Sundays. It was not your responsibility to save this guy. We can all do more witnessing, but people have to take responsibility for themselves. The Lord knocked on Drake's door several times, but he refused to answer."

When we were at the graveside, I kept noticing that it was a beautiful day. The sky was perfectly still and there was a slight breeze.

I stood still and thought as the clouds rolled by slowly, *This is the beginning, Payton. Now you know the importance of making sure everyone you know has a personal relationship with God. Don't let another opportunity pass you by. Don't have another day like this. Look around you. There are plenty of people who need God. It won't be easy, but it will be rewarding.*

A big smile came across my face. I noticed Hayli looking very sad when it was time to leave the cemetery. The Spirit told me I needed to give her comfort.

I walked up and grabbed her hand. It was as if she had a lot balled up, and she released it all to me.

Thank You, Lord. Thanks for using me, I thought as I looked up to the sky.

"Payton, I'll miss him forever."

"I know. But think about how much better his life was because you were in it."

I wanted to do more and say more, but for that moment it was enough. When another opportunity arose, I was going to seize it for God.

"Are you sure you don't mind?" I asked Tad a few days later on the phone when I was back at school.

"No. You and Dakari are just friends and I trust you. He needs both of us right now. If his mom wants you to come and help clean out some of Drake's things and you're fine with that, then I'm fine too."

I was still uneasy about being around the Grahams during this crisis. I didn't really have the words to say to them, but I knew the Lord would equip me with all I needed to say. When Dakari asked me if I would help, I told him I would. However, I did want to clear it with my boyfriend first, and I was thankful that Tad understood.

I thanked Tad for his sweet understanding and told him that I would call him when I came back to school. Dakari and I were planning to head to Augusta right after classes on Thursday. I still couldn't believe he was back at school the day after the funeral. He told Tad that he needed to keep busy, and staying in the house wasn't going to be easy for him.

"Why did it have to be like this?" Dakari asked me in the car. "I called my brother's cell phone all week hoping he would answer, but he's gone. It's like he's disappeared. Now my mom wants to get rid of all of his stuff. I thought I was strong, but . . ."

"Why don't you pull over and let me drive," I said to my emotional friend.

"That's a good idea," Dakari admitted as he pulled the car off the road.

"Dakari, you know God wouldn't have wanted—"

"Payton, you know I'm not wantin' to hear all that. Tad been layin' the same stuff down on me."

When we got to Augusta, I started en route to Dakari's home.

"No, we're not going there," he said as he handed me a piece of paper. "Here are the directions."

"Directions to where?"

"To the attorney's office."

"For what?"

"They are reading my brother's will."

A lump developed in my throat. Why in the world would Dakari want me at the will reading?

"Why are you taking me with you? This is family stuff," I told him.

"My mom said your name is in the will."

"What? Why?"

"I don't know. That's why we're going to find out."

Thirty minutes later we were sitting in the lawyer's office. The Grahams had embraced me and thanked me for my support.

The will reading was shocking. "Hayli, thank you for loving me all these years. I want 75 percent of what I have to go to you and our children. Little brother, you've got spunk so I want you and your wife, Payton, to have the other 25 percent. Just in case Hayli and I don't get married, or if we get a divorce, give Dakari 75 and Hayli 25. Dakari, use this money wisely. Make sure you go and put fresh flowers on Mama and Daddy's graves."

I think all of us were shocked about the details of the will. The majority of Drake's signing bonus went to Dakari.

"Sir, this can't be right," Dakari spoke as everyone else was silent. "My parents aren't even in there."

"I tried to tell your brother that," Mr. Boulder said. "He never foresaw himself dying before your parents. This will shall stand unless contested. That's the way he wanted it to be."

"No, that's not the way he wanted it to be. He wouldn't want my parents left without anything."

"Well, the money is there for you to do whatever you want with it."

"Mom, Dad, say something."

"Say what, Dakari? Drake has spoken and we want to honor that. We don't need the money."

"Yeah, but I'm in college. I don't know anything about managing money. Dad!"

"Son, I will work with you on a financial plan. Hayli, we consider you our daughter. Now the wedding expenses can be paid off."

"I'd rather have Drake than his money."

"I know. That's probably why he left you something, because he knew that too."

Later, at the Grahams' house, Dakari and I were in Drake's room packing.

Dakari grabbed my hand and said, "You are beautiful."

"Thanks," I said as I went back to packing.

"Payton, you heard my brother's will. We need to be together. That's what my brother wanted and what I always wanted. I can provide for us."

"Dakari, don't make me do this with you right now."

"Are you scared to tell Tad you don't want to be with him? You don't have a problem telling me."

"Tad may not have twenty million dollars, but he has my heart. I love him."

"If you love him, then why are you here with me?"

"Because I'm your friend and I care about you. I'm sorry that your brother is gone. I know how much you cared for him. I'm grateful that he showed you how much he loved you. His way of doing things is not my way. I don't want to be with you, Dakari."

"Things won't be the way they were, Payton. I'm ready to settle down."

"I'm ready to settle down, too, and Tad and I are just fine."

"Fine, you can go back. I've got Drake's ride."

"Oh, the Ferrari is yours?"

"Don't worry about all that, Payton. Just go!"

"I thought you needed my help."

"Just go. Didn't you hear me? If you don't want to be my girl, then fine. There are plenty of ladies that want me. You're gonna wish you hadn't turned me down."

"I'm sorry you feel that way, Dakari. I thought we could still be friends. If you find that you need a friend, you can find me back at school."

As I headed out, Dakari's parents asked me why I was leaving so early. They had prepared dinner and wanted to talk to me. I told them I needed to get back to school. They told me they understood and appreciated my being there.

The ride home was miserable. It was very dreary and the sprinkles of rain made it hard to see. I hoped the fog would lift soon. That was also the case for my hopes with Dakari. I hoped he would soon get over his dampening mood. I was thankful God had given me wisdom to see through what was deeper with Dakari at that moment. Although I wanted him to feel better, I was not the one to carry his heart.

My cell phone rang just as I approached Athens. It was Dakari's mom.

"Payton, are you all right on that dark road?"

"Yeah. I'm almost back at school."

"I just wanted to check on you and tell you again how much I appreciate you. Please keep the things disclosed in my son's will confidential."

"I will. I understand. I'll be praying for you and your family, and if there is anything my family or I can do, please call on us."

"We will. Your mom has been bringing food by here every day. Do you cook like her, girl?"

"No."

"Well, you better get down from Athens and get in her kitchen and learn."

"All right. Tell everyone good-bye for me."

"OK, 'bye."

As I put my cell phone in my lap, I prayed aloud, "Lord, please bless the Graham family. They are hurting and they need You. Give them peace, especially Dakari. Amen."

"Knock, knock," I said through the bathroom door to Jewels and Robyn's room.

I was glad Jewels wasn't there. Robyn was under the covers and it was only 8:30.

"What's wrong with you?" I asked.

120

"It's not like I have a date or anything to go on. You're the one with all the men," she replied.

"What's that supposed to mean?" I asked her.

"Nothing."

"Robyn, something is bothering you, but you seem a little short, and I've had too long a day to worry about it."

"OK." She sat up and said. "I'm sorry, but I'm depressed."

"About what?"

"You wouldn't understand."

"Robyn, I've been depressed about men. I realized that the man I needed in my heart, I had all the time. All I had to do was let the Spirit lead me. The Grahams are depressed. Their son is dead and he is never coming back. You have no reason to be depressed."

"Oh, yeah, speaking of which," Robyn said as if she was about to share more bad news, "Laurel's gone."

"What do you mean? Gone where?"

"Her grandfather is really sick and her mother suggested she take a week from school and go to Arkansas. They don't expect him to live for more than a few days. She left the number in your room."

"How was she?"

"Not too good."

"Robyn, that's what I mean. Your situation could always be worse."

I knew I needed to be a friend to Robyn and not judge her. We stayed up all night and talked about how sad she still was that she and Jackson weren't together. I told her she didn't need him. All she needed was Christ. We grew closer as we talked about God.

The phone rang and I quickly answered it.

"Are you up?" Tad asked.

"Yeah. What are you doing up?"

"I'm on my way to class. Dakari's not here so I wanted to check in on you."

"I'm sorry I didn't get to call you. I was wondering if you could pray for my day," I said to him.

"Sure, Payton. Heavenly Father, I ask you to bless my girlfriend. Take what is wrong and make it right. I pray she takes whatever is weighing down on her and put it in Your hands. Amen."

"Thank you. It's weird how you can read my mind. I'll see you later, OK?"

"Are you feeling better?"

"Yes, thank you, Tad."

When I put down the phone, I looked at the number Laurel had left and decided to call.

"Payton, hey! I didn't expect you to call this soon."

"I just wanted to let you know that I'm sorry to hear about your grandfather. But until God calls him, we still have hope for a miracle."

"You're so right. Now that my grandfather has accepted the Lord, it makes me feel a lot better about God's will. I know that this life isn't the end for either of us. It was sweet of you to call."

"Make sure you tell your grandfather all you want to say."

"Thanks. I will. You quit worrying about me and make sure you practice those flips."

"I was thinking about not trying out."

"Payton! You can't do that. But to be honest, so was I."

Laurel and I made a deal that we would help each other and at least try to get it together for tryouts.

"Tell your family that I'm praying for them, all right?"

"OK. 'Bye, Payton."

I only had a few minutes to get ready for class. I thought about all the people who meant so much to me. All of my friends were going through a lot, but I wasn't God, and I couldn't solve their problems. My only job was to make sure I was caring for friends.

10

Tripping Over Everything

irl, you're so funny," I said to Laurel as I watched her try to mimic the dance I was teaching her a week later. "You know, with floor routines, I thought you had to know how to dance."

"The balance beam was my best event, Payton. There's just no hope," she said, getting frustrated.

"You've got hope, Laurel. You can hear the music, can't you? Just let the music take over."

Laurel had only been back to school for two days since being in Arkansas. Sadly, her grandfather passed. We had talked about how this was affecting her, and when she described the funeral to me, it reminded me of my grandfather's service just a few months before. We had already said that we were going to help each other get ready for cheerleading, but now we had a much bigger mission, which was to keep each other encouraged.

"OK, Payton. Enough picking on me."

"I'm not picking on you, Laurel. You've got to get this."

"OK, since you think it's that easy to learn a dance, let me see you do a round-off back handspring."

"That's not fair," I told her.

"Well, you've at least got to try. What's wrong, Payton? Need me to spot you?"

"Yes."

I was so nervous that when I went into the flip, I tripped over my own feet. "I can't do this," I said, frustrated.

"Well, now you see how I feel, Payton. Tryouts are at the end of the month. We need a miracle," she said as she sat down beside me.

"I guess we'll have to keep praying for one."

As we walked back to our dorm, I said, "Gosh, it's hard not talking to Tad."

"You still haven't talked to him? It's been four days. What's going on?" Laurel asked.

"Tomorrow's April Fool's, and I'm playing a joke on him."

"Are you serious? What's the joke?"

After I told her everything, she said I was completely wrong for playing the joke on Tad. She suggested that I not play with fire because I might be the one to get burned.

When I got home, there were two messages on the machine from Tad, and his voice sounded urgent. I was excited because I knew the joke was going to work. Last year in high school he and my rival, Starr Love, got me good. She told me that she kissed him and I went off on him. When he told me it was a joke, I vowed to get him back. Every twenty minutes I looked at the clock because at 12:01, I was going to dial Tad up.

Later in the evening my alarm clock went off. It was 11:50. I must have dozed off.

"Payton," Laurel said as she rolled over, still tired. "You're not gonna do that to the boy, are you?"

"Girl, go back to sleep."

"I would hate for this to backfire on you."

"It'll be fine. Tad is a big practical joker. He will under-stand."

At 12:01 I dialed Tad's number. The machine came on.

"Tad," I said, "this is Payton. I know I haven't talked to you in a few days, but I've been thinking about us and things are getting too—"

"Payton, what's up? I was asleep," Tad said as he answered the phone.

"I'm sorry to bother you, Tad, but I think you demand too much from me. Maybe this commitment thing is too much."

"What are you tryin' to say? Do you want to break up? If you don't think you want to be with me, I can give you some space."

"Well, that's what I want," I told him nonchalantly.

"Are you sayin' we're breakin' up or somethin'?"

"Yeah, Tad."

I couldn't tell how this was affecting him, but his silence was scaring me. Could this backfire on me?

"Tad, are you OK? You're not saying anything."

"What do you want me to say?"

"Are you all right?"

"Yeah. Good night," he said as he hung up the phone.

"Oh my goodness!" I said loudly.

"What happened?" Laurel asked.

"He just hung up on me."

"Well, what did you expect him to do? You just broke up with him."

"He was supposed to try and get me to change my mind. Then I was going to say, 'April Fool's.'"

"Payton, I told you you were playing with fire."

"I've got to call him back and explain."

"Don't. It's midnight."

"I need to call him back so he won't be upset."

"He's upset because you called him early in the morning

and told him that stuff in the first place. Wait until morning. He will be thinking more clearly then."

"Maybe you're right."

I got down on my knees and prayed, *I hope I didn't ruin things for us. It was just a joke. Make him understand.*

I got into bed, but I couldn't believe this. It was supposed to be a joke, but it turned out to be a big mess. Hopefully Laurel was right and I could fix this in the morning. However, the morning wasn't coming soon enough so I started naming the books of the Bible.

"Genesis, Exodus, Leviticus, Numbers, Deuteronomy, Joshua, Judges, Ruth, 1 Samuel, 2 Samuel, 1 Kings, 2 Kings, 1 Chronicles, 2 Chronicles, Ezra, Nehemiah, Esther, Job, Psalms, Proverbs, Ecclesiastes, Song of Songs, Isaiah, Jeremiah, Lamentations, Ezekiel, Daniel, Hosea, Joel, Amos, Obadiah, Jonah, Micah, Nahum, Habukkuk, Zephaniah, Haggai, Zechariah, Malachi, Matthew, Mark, Luke . . ."

Luke was the last thing I remember saying. I fell asleep in hopes of a better day tomorrow.

"Payton! You're gonna be late to class! It's 9:30!" Laurel screamed in my ear, attempting to wake me up.

"Oh my gosh! I'm already late!"

"April Fool's! It's only 8:00!"

"Oh, you're so wrong!" I exclaimed as I bopped her with my pillow.

"Ouch!" she said. "Well, that's what you get. You said you liked practical jokes."

"Yeah, but I didn't know you did too."

"I got you."

"Do you think Tad is really mad at me?" I asked.

"I don't know, but that was a cruel joke. If I had a boyfriend I wouldn't want him to play that type of joke on me.

I would probably be mad for a long time."

"Would you really? It was just a joke."

"Yeah, but not everything is funny. I'm sure that once you explain it to him, Tad will understand."

"I sure hope so."

I dialed Tad's number but got his answering machine. I wanted to talk to him in person so I hung up.

I knew his first class was far from mine, but I didn't care. I didn't want the day starting off with him thinking we had broken up.

Maybe he was in the shower, I thought. *I'll call one more time.*

This time Dakari picked up. "Hello? Hello? I know somebody is there. Don't make me star-69 you," he threatened when I didn't say anything.

"It's me, Dakari."

"Your boy ain't here. Or are you callin' me?"

"Dakari—"

"Don't Dakari me. Who do you want to speak to? Pretty soon I'm gonna be the only one at Georgia anyway, but you didn't hear that from me."

"What are you talkin' about?"

"There's a letter here from Duke to Tad."

"What do you mean?"

"They are checkin' Tad out. Since the coaches have changed, any player is free to go, and Tad might."

"Did Tad tell you he was thinking about this?"

"No, I just saw the letter. He doesn't know I read it or anything."

"Why are you reading his mail?"

"Oh, please. It's not a big deal. I thought it was mine."

"So what did it say exactly?" I said in a disappointed tone.

"First you didn't want me to read his mail, and now you want me to tell you what it says. You can't have it both ways, baby. You ask him. But he ain't here."

"Well, how are you?"

"I'm fine. I'm cool," he said.

I knew him, and I knew he was fronting, trying to have thick skin so he wouldn't let on that he was still hurting.

"I'm a little ticked at my mom because she's trippin'. She got me walkin'."

"You don't have a car?"

"No. Mine's in the shop and she won't bring Dra—my new ride up here."

I could tell it was hard for him to even mention his brother's name.

"Well, I'm gonna let you go, but if you need a ride somewhere let me know."

Through the course of the conversation, Laurel had gone. I thought about Dakari, and him still dealing with everything. He was dealing with it on his own. He wasn't seeking God anywhere and that had to be destructive. All I could do was think about that old Helen Baylor song "Can You Reach My Friend?" Even though I couldn't sing, I hummed the words to the best of my ability. I just wanted the Lord to hear my plea.

I prayed, "Can You reach my friend? You're the only one who can. I know You love him. Help him understand You. Can you reach my friend? Bring his searching to an end. Help him give his heart to You. As bad as Dakari wants to see his brother, I pray that he never sees him again. If he doesn't accept You, he's going straight to hell. Don't let that happen, Lord. Do whatever You have to do to let him know he needs You. Please fix this thing with me and Tad. Amen."

An hour later, I was in front of Tad's first-period class. "Hey," I said when I saw him walking to his classroom.

"What are you doing here?" he asked coldly.

"I wanted to talk to you."

"Well, you said it all last night."

"Last night I was just—"

"Payton, you don't have to check on me. I'm all right. I

can move on now. I cared about you, but I'm fine without you."

He walked around me, not allowing me to say anything. I wanted to follow him, but I didn't have time because I had to get to class too.

Before I could leave his building he came back up to me and said, "Coach Mullens and his wife wanted us to sit with the babies. I just wanted to know if that was OK with you."

"Yeah, that's fine."

"I'll meet you there."

"We can ride together, Tad."

"Why go through all that? Let's just make a clean break of our relationship. Best wishes for your cheerleading try-outs today."

"Tad, wait."

"Payton, I don't want to talk about our relationship. It's over."

"No, it's not about that. Are you changing schools?"

"Where did you get that from?"

"Dakari."

"We'll talk tonight," he told me, avoiding my question.

I arrived late to my class. I hoped that I hadn't messed things up with Tad for good. I hated having to go through the day with Tad thinking we were apart, but fortunately I could set things straight this evening by baby-sitting the twins who were our namesakes. I hoped so anyway.

It was about four o'clock and there was a gym filled with men and women wanting to try out for cheerleader. It was the first day of the three-week process. This meeting was for information, and there were so many people in the bleachers I couldn't find Laurel.

Maybe she decided not to try out, I thought.

Then I heard her say, "Excuse me," while tripping over someone's feet. She nervously sat beside me.

The cheerleading sponsor got up to talk first. "Being a Georgia Bulldog cheerleader is a great honor. We take pride in what we do. We go to competitions because, like the players we cheer for, we like to win. We will have fourteen cheerleaders on the squad. Seven boys and seven girls. We will also have a mascot. Tryouts this year will be tough. We have two rounds. Those who make it through the first round will go on to the second round, and those who make it through the second round will make the team. Our returning cheerleaders are exempt from our first round, but it is not guaranteed that they will make it again."

Laurel held out her hand and I placed mine in hers. We held hands tightly. Both of us were thinking the same thing. There was probably less than a one-percent chance that we would both make the team.

"Last year's squad will be teaching you the first round. We will bring in a choreographer for the second round. Without further ado, I'm going to bring out last year's squad to show you what you will be practicing. Bring out the dogs!"

As I watched the cheerleaders, I only saw one person who looked like me, and he was a man. When they did their hurkies, toe touches, splits, double somersaults, dances, and cheers, I was in awe. There was no way I could make the squad.

"I hope you guys are fired up by what you saw," the sponsor told us as he looked around the crowd. "We'll see you here tomorrow promptly at 4:00. Dress in a red shirt, black shorts, white socks, and white tennis shoes."

"Well," I said to Laurel on the way home, "I'm going to do my part in making sure you know the dance. I just need to get *you* on the team."

"What are you talking about, Payton? You have a better

131

chance of making the team than I do. You've already done cheerleading in high school. I would rather put all my energy into you."

"Laurel, you're white, so you have a better chance."

"Stop using that race stuff."

"It's true."

"Well, if anything, you have a better shot because they know they need to diversify. However, neither one of us can quit. We've got to give it all we've got. If one of us makes the squad, it will count as a victory for both of us. We both know the Lord and He will produce a miracle."

We went from believing that neither of us was going to make the team to knowing that both of us were going to. The Lord was on our side, and with Him all things are possible. We now had the faith we lacked before. It didn't matter what the odds looked like. We knew we would come out of the fight. We had faith. We had each other. We had God.

"Are you sure you guys know what to do?" Shayna asked, going through the list with Tad and me for the twelfth time.

Her husband was as cool as a cucumber. "They've got it. These kids are responsible."

"I know. I just wanted to make sure they know everything about the babies. Skky likes to listen to 'Joybells' and Taylor doesn't care too much. I need to teach you guys baby CPR."

"Joybells? What's that?" I asked.

"Oh, it's this adorable new kids gospel group. Look at the CD."

I smiled at the four cute faces on the cover.

"Shayna, get out of here," I told her half-jokingly.

"We'll be fine," Tad assured her.

"We're just going to dinner and a movie and we'll be

right back," she told us.

I wanted to tell her to quit tripping, but I realized that these were her babies and, if I was in her shoes, I'd probably be stressed to the max as well.

As soon as they left I tried talking to Tad, but he wasn't hearing what I wanted to say. He kept trying to straighten up, but he had no idea what he was doing.

"I want to talk to you. Why are you avoiding me?"

"Because it seems like you're trying to make me feel better. It's OK. I'm just trying to figure out if I want to go to Duke in the summer or wait until the fall."

"You're going?"

"Yeah."

"You know Coach Mullens is here."

"Coach Mullens isn't going to let me start. Rocky is coming and we already have too many running backs. Since you and I are not going to be together anymore, I have decided to go for my dreams at another school."

I went over to the window and tears started to drip from my face. How could he give up on us? Our relationship was worth fighting for.

"Why the tears?"

"I can't believe you're willing to give up so easily. It was just a joke. I love you."

I felt arms around my waist, and he whispered in my ear, "I knew it was a joke all along. April Fool's on you."

"What?" I turned and asked as I hit him softly in the chest. "You knew, and all day you made me think we were broken up?"

"Yeah. I'm not going to Duke either. Gotcha twice. You know Coach Mullens wasn't going to let me go anywhere."

"But Dakari found the letter."

"Duke asked me to come, so I left the letter out. I knew Dakari would tell you about it."

"You planned to fool me with this moving thing?"

133

"Yeah, but you scared me first when you called last night. Or should I say this morning? I knew whatever you said had to be linked with April Fool's, but I wanted to beat you at your own game. Now come here. I want to hold my girlfriend."

It felt good being in his arms. He really did care about me. He wasn't giving up on our relationship, and he didn't plan on going to some school miles away. Tad Taylor was still my guy and though he had beaten me at some April Fool's trick, I was happy we were still together.

Before we could say it to each other Skky started to cry. I tried to calm her down, but she wouldn't stop. Tad thought he could help, but when he was about to try, Taylor started screaming. The two of us were going crazy trying to handle the babies.

"We need bottles," Tad said. "How do we make the formula?"

"It's ready to serve. Just pop open the can and pour it into the bottle. Weren't you listening?"

"I thought you were."

With babies crying and us bickering, it was eventful but fun. The night was topped off when Tad went to change Taylor and he checked him a little too soon.

"You got squirted." I laughed. "I guess that was Taylor's April Fool's trick on you."

"Why are you giving me a hard time?"

"Because you deserve it."

We couldn't stop laughing. As I looked back over the day's events, I realized that it's good not to take life too seriously. It was actually fun tripping over everything.

11

Going
Up North

Tad and I had a great time baby-sitting the twins. They settled down and we tidied up, but I couldn't understand why Tad had such a sad look on his face.

Instead of instantly getting upset, I just prayed. *Lord, something is obviously not right. I don't know what's wrong with my boyfriend, but I don't want him going through any drama. He knows we can talk about anything, but he's not opening up. Help him talk to me, Lord. If he does, give me Your words to share.*

"What? Why are you looking at me like that?" Tad asked as he noticed the concerned look on my face.

"I'm worried about you."

"Don't be. I was just thinking about Dakari, that's all."

I found that odd. Here we were having a wonderful time, and he was thinking about my ex. Dakari was his roommate, so I guess he was entitled.

"Pay, the brother is struggling. He won't talk to me. He doesn't even know his worth in Christ. He's been moping around, but I know he's got a lot going on. He is in trouble with the coach. I'm trying to reach out, but he won't let me in."

"It's got to be tough for you."

"Yeah," he said, "seeing the brother struggle. He is not ready. He is not on his knees. He is too strong to be weak, or so he thinks."

"Maybe we need to pray for God to show him mercy."

"I've been doing that. I've been lifting him up to the Lord constantly."

"Let's try it together. You were the one who showed me that a relationship is only strong if it is built on Christ. I care for him too."

"Yeah, I know. He's starting to think he doesn't have anything. I've been where he is. That's why I follow the Lord like I do."

"You never told me what happened to make you such a good Christian."

"Baby, my family life was rough. I had a lot of anger built up. I was mad at God for allowing my dad to hurt my mom. God broke me when I came to Him for help in dealing with my anger. I think that is the only thing that can change Dakari. I know we can't change his heart, but God can."

I went over, grabbed his hands, and took him to the Mullenses' living room floor, where I prayed. "Lord, we ask that You help our friend Dakari. He lost his brother and he feels like he doesn't have anything. He thinks he doesn't need You. You are so holy, Lord. Please help us get through to Dakari. Bless his heart, Lord. Break him so You can bless him. Use Tad to help Dakari. Help Dakari break free and see You in his heart as clearly as Tad and I see You. We love You and praise You. Amen."

"Thanks," Tad said.

"For what?"

"For taking the lead. I was so frustrated. I needed that prayer as much as Dakari. You were selfless and there for me. I appreciate it."

"No problem. I love you and know what that really means. I want to do my part to make you the best man God wants you to be. You lifted me up for so long. It's time for me to carry my weight in our relationship."

"Thank you for being my girl and telling Dakari it was me and you. That's why I trusted you to go to Augusta with him. I knew there was nothing he could do to sway you back under his spell."

"He did try. He had some things that he thought I wanted, but in no way could they compare to you. I love you," I said, placing my hands firmly on his face.

The Mullenses came in from their date and found things in order. Tad and I smiled at each other because we knew things weren't always peaceful in their home. We had done it. It was a great evening and a joyful April Fool's Day that I would always remember.

———————

I felt like I was a gymnast as many times as I was doing those back handsprings.

As soon as I finished my classes, I headed over to the gymnastics building. Though Laurel wasn't on the team anymore, her old coach still allowed her to practice in the gym.

Laurel was getting better at the cheers and dances. I was getting better at the back handsprings. Now we had a legitimate shot at making the squad. After I finished one of my flips, there were claps coming from the door.

"Oh, look who's here," Laurel teased.

Tad was standing at the door with a blond-haired dude who was unfamiliar to me.

"I know that guy," Laurel said in my ear.

"Who is he?"

"He's a cheerleader."

What would Tad be doing with a cheerleader? I wondered.

"Hey, love," he said sweetly.

"What are you doing here?" I questioned.

"I came for support. Hey, Laurel," Tad said to my room-mate. "I want to introduce you to someone. This is Gordon."

"Aren't you a cheerleader?" Laurel asked.

"Yeah," he answered. "How are y'all doing? It looks like you're working hard."

"What are you doing here?" I questioned Tad again.

"Gordon is here to help you guys with your stunts because you don't have them down yet."

"I'd love to help you practice," Gordon put in.

"Is that legal?" Laurel asked with concern.

"Yes. I can work with you and teach you some stunts because it is required that you know them for tryouts."

"What? Why are you looking at me like that?" Tad asked. "Don't you want to work with Gordon?"

"I don't know. How can I ever repay you for working with us?" I asked Gordon.

"It's not about paying me back. There needs to be some diversity on the squad. I'm willing to do my part to make sure we get some. We can even practice during spring break."

"That would be great!" Laurel exclaimed.

I wasn't so sure. I hadn't made plans for spring break, but I certainly knew I didn't want to stay in Athens.

"You two have a chance, but you've got to practice hard."

"I still don't understand," I said "Why would you want to help us? We're complete strangers."

"My stubborn girlfriend," Tad said jokingly. "She always thinks about the worst things."

I got frustrated with Tad and walked away. He came up behind me and said, "What's wrong with you?"

"I wonder if he would be so willing to help me if my boyfriend didn't play football here. I don't want any special favors just because I'm your girlfriend. I want to make the squad on my own abilities."

"So what if I know a few people? The world revolves around who you know."

"Well, I know God and I've been praying for Him to help me make the team. If I make it, it will be because He wants me to."

"Why can't you look at this as God allowing me to get someone to teach you some skills that you don't know so you can make it? Why can't it be working out like that? Don't block your blessings. You asked God to help you and He sent this guy. I don't think he knows the Lord so maybe you can repay him by teaching him something about God."

"I'm sorry," I said to him. "I'm just not used to people helping me like this. I don't think I deserve it."

"Don't take my love and throw it back in my face. You don't have to earn it. I want to love you like God loves me, unconditionally. Accept my gift and Gordon's help."

I went back and started practicing with Gordon and Laurel. Both of the times Gordon lifted Laurel up, she fell to the ground. This was going to take a lot of work.

"Why are y'all puttin' the pressure on me?" I said, talking to my three high school girlfriends on a conference call.

It was good talking to Rain, Lynzi, and Dymond. It had been a long time since we had gabbed together. But just because I wasn't going along with the plan they had come up with, I was the bad guy. "I'm not driving all the way up to D.C. I'm trying out for cheerleader."

"So don't spoil the fun. You cheered in high school. Are tryouts the same week as the one we're talking about?" asked Dymond.

"No, they're the week we get back."

"Well, you're not going to miss nothin'," Dymond said.

"How are things at Howard?" I asked, trying to relieve some of the tension.

"If you came up here, you would find out. We're having a lot of slammin' parties this weekend. You know you need to be up here," Dymond bragged.

"Dymond, I kind of have things going on with my new boyfriend," Rain interjected, "I wanna come, but the whole week might be a bit much."

"I finally got leave time from the army and y'all are goin' to act like this?" Lynzi said. "Are you choosing cheerleading and your boyfriends over us?"

"Lynzi, you have a car. Why don't you come down here?" I asked.

"My car is not as new as yours. I can't take it on that long drive."

"Well, I'm not asking my parents," I told them.

"Don't ask. Just go," Lynzi suggested.

"What if something happens and I get into trouble? Maybe we can fly up there and stay for a couple of days," I suggested.

"I can plan around, maybe," Dymond announced.

"Lynzi," I said, "if you don't want to drive or fly then maybe you should take the bus."

"Payton, don't worry about what I do. If we see you and Rain in D.C. then that's cool. If not, that's cool too." When I hung up the phone, it rang again.

"Hello?" I said, agitated.

"Girl, I can't believe them," Rain said, letting me know that she felt the same way I did. "They were trying to make us feel guilty."

"Let's be bigger than that and pray."

"I'm too mad to pray. I wanna spend some time with my boyfriend. I miss the girls, but I want to go down to Savannah with some of the other students from the AUC."

"I don't know what I'm going to do, either, but if we do go, maybe we can fly up together for real."

"That sounds good."

"I'll talk to my parents and call you back tomorrow."

As soon as I hung up, I started praying. *Lord, high school is over and I want to maintain my friendship with my girls. Help them to understand that I have a life, and help them support me. Help me to be sensitive to them. Work it out, please. Give me a clean heart, Lord. I want to serve You. I need Your strength. I love You. Come into my life, Lord. Amen.*

"Dang, you're cute," the black male cheerleader Willie said to me.

Laurel and Gordon were practicing their stunt and Willie was going on and on about how he loved gymnastics.

He was such a pretty boy with yellow skin and wavy hair. When he put me in the air, it was as if he was feeling on me instead of doing his job.

"Stop! Put me down!" I yelled.

"What's the problem?"

"Don't hold my butt like that!" I yelled louder.

Laurel and Gordon came over to us.

"I'm supposed to hold you like that. How else do you think you'll get lifted in the air?"

"You don't have to rub on it!"

"I wasn't," he responded.

Laurel pulled me to the side and asked, "What's going on? The're just trying to help us make the squad. Don't start anything."

"You don't even know what he did to me."

"What did he do?"

"Why do I have to explain to defend myself? You don't understand, Laurel. He was rubbing on my behind."

141

"I don't need to help her," Willie yelled out to Gordon, "I'm going to make the squad again!"

"You know what? I don't even want your services anymore! I'm through practicing for today," I said as I got ready to leave.

With all the frustration I had inside, I knew it was time for me to take a break from cheerleading. It had been the only thing I spent my time on. Maybe going up to Howard was what I needed to relax. I had had enough and needed a break.

I was getting ready to walk out the gym door when Willie came up to me and said, "We need to put all this stuff aside. I was just trying to help you out. You didn't have to go off on me. Sistahs are always trippin'."

"What does this have to do with my skin color? If anything, I would have thought a brother would be on my side."

"Gordon told me your boyfriend plays on the football team, but he's a freshman and I'm a junior."

"And? So what? Who cares?"

"I've been doing this for years. I'm just trying to help the only way I know how. I can teach you all you need to know if you give me a chance."

I wanted to slap him. I couldn't believe what he was doing. I walked away as Tad entered the gym.

"What's going on?" Tad asked as he came between Willie and me. "Payton, are you all right?"

"I don't know," I answered with frustration.

"What's up, man? What are you doing to my girl?"

"I'm just trying to help. You want her to make the squad. You enlisted my help."

"No, I enlisted Gordon's help. I don't even know you. Gordon, come here!" Tad yelled.

Gordon turned pink as he and Laurel walked toward the three of us.

"What's up here, Gordon?"

He was silent, so Laurel offered all the information she knew.

"Payton, what do you mean he touched you the wrong way?" Tad asked, stepping closer to Willie.

"Gordon asked me to help and that's all I was doing."

"Payton never asked for your help, Willie. How could you disrespect her and me like this," he questioned Willie with disgust in his voice.

"Look, freshman, it's cute that you want your girl to make the squad and all, but she needs some help. I can help her."

Gordon jumped in. "I asked Willie to help because I didn't have enough time to teach both Laurel and Payton. Willie's really good at gymnastics. I think it's all a misunderstanding."

"OK, maybe I overreacted," I stated, reevaluating my position.

"Let's go," Tad said.

"She ain't gonna make the squad if y'all leave," Willie said.

"I'm tired now. I need a break."

When Tad and I got to the door he said, "Wait one second at the car. I'll be right back."

He got straight into Willie's face. I don't know what he said, but Willie came over to me and made sure I knew he was sorry for giving me the wrong impression before he quickly exited.

"He's cool."

"Yeah, maybe, but I'm tired of cheering. In a couple of days I'm going to D.C."

"Why?"

"I want to hang with Dymond and Lynzi. I think Rain and I are going to fly up there. Maybe when I come back I'll have a better attitude."

"That's cool. I'll see you when you get back."

Later that night I called my parents. "Hey, Mommy. I love you and I miss you."

"Payton Skky, what do you want?"

"Why do you think I want something? I just decided to take some time off with Rain to go see Dymond in D.C."

"Dymond's mom called me and said she was worried about her. She hadn't heard from her in a while. When are you planning to go and how long are you planning to stay?"

"Just for the weekend."

"That's long enough. Is Dymond going to pick you up from the airport?"

"I'm sure she'll have no problem with that. Do you think Dad will be OK with this?"

"Yeah, he should. How is cheerleading going?"

"The routines are hard."

"You can do it, sweetie."

"Thanks for believing in me, Mom."

"All right. Call me back with your plans."

When I got off the phone with my mom I was excited. I was heading to D.C. and was going to have a wonderful time.

"No, I do not want to go on a date with those guys. I didn't come up here to hang with them. They've been smoking that stuff," I exclaimed.

"You're right, Payton. You should have stayed in Georgia because you're ruining all the fun!" Lynzi exclaimed.

"I don't feel comfortable with it either," Rain said. "We don't even know them."

Dymond and Lynzi wanted us to ride in a van to Maryland with four guys from Bowie State that we didn't even know. It wasn't safe. If I had known that they would be trippin' like this, I would have stayed in Athens.

"Anything could happen," I told them. "At my school, a girl went on a date and her date killed her."

"What if they rape you?" I asked. "What is going on with you guys? Ever since Rain and I got here y'all have had attitudes. My plane leaves in twelve hours. I can take a standby and leave early if I have to."

"Then take your stuff and leave," Dymond said, pointing to the door. "What's stopping you?"

I called a cab. I was willing to wait at the airport all night before I went to Maryland with four guys I didn't know. "If y'all want to party with them strangers then go ahead. I'll be praying for you, but I fear the Lord and I know His plan for my life don't include those men!"

Dymond kicked my suitcase toward the door. "Get your bag and get out. You are so judgmental and I'm sick of it. You think you are the only one who is ever right."

"I have never said that."

"Get your stuff and go, Payton! Rain, you get out too!"

My friend grabbed her stuff and walked out the door while I followed.

We sat in the airport in silence. I was very frustrated with my life. It was like most of the world had lost its mind.

Just as I was about to pray, Rain said, "Are you mad?"

"No, I'm cool."

"I'm mad. I'm never coming back here again."

"I love going up North."

"Why? It was a disaster!"

"I call talking to Jesus 'going up North.'"

12

Realizing the Dilemma

O h my gosh!" I said when I got to my car in the Atlanta airport parking lot and I realized I did not have my keys.

I had packed in a haste to leave D.C. I guess I'd forgotten my car keys.

"This is just great!" I yelled as I kicked the tire. "How are we supposed to get home?"

"It's OK. Let's calm down and think about it," Rain said.

"I know my dad has another set at the dealership in Augusta, but what should I say? I can't tell him the truth about what happened and why we're back so early or he'll freak out. This is such a big mess."

I had a lot of anger bottled up inside. I was so frustrated. I thought I was cool and that I had given it all to God, but I was still bummed out.

"Come on. You can come to my dorm room and call your dad."

Rain used my cell phone to call her boyfriend, Jordan,

to pick us up. She got through to him, but he had loaned his car to his roommate.

"So when is Randy coming back?" I heard her say. "What do you mean you're not sure? Is he supposed to be an hour or what? Oh, that's not bad. We can wait twenty minutes. We'll be by the Delta baggage claim waiting at the curb. I miss you too. 'Bye."

She handed me the phone with a humungous smile plastered across her face. I never thought she would smile like that after she broke up with Tyson. I was glad Rain was happy.

"Do you want me to call your parents for you?" Rain asked.

"No. Then they'll be mad at both of us. You didn't remember to bring the keys either."

"I would have brought them, but I didn't know you left them."

"I'm just kidding, Rain." I sighed. "I'll call them."

I had to spend about fifteen minutes talking to my parents about the situation. Everyone was extremely busy, so how I was going to get the keys was anybody's guess. My dad was going on and on about responsibility, but since I had already beaten myself up about that, I told him I would figure something out and call him back. He appreciated my adult response and agreed to let me try and handle it.

"Why don't you just call Tad?" Rain suggested.

"He's got training, and he was not too happy to hear about me going to D.C."

"Payton, just call the man."

I dialed the digits and almost bit my lip when Dakari picked up.

Why me? I thought.

"Is your roommate in?" I asked.

"Oh, I don't get a hello or anything, huh? If you can't respect me, then I'm not going to pass him the phone."

Tad must have heard Dakari giving me a hard time because he got on the phone and said, "Hello."

"Hey, I miss you," I said honestly.

"I miss you too. What's up?"

"I'm at the Atlanta airport and I left my keys in D.C. No one can bring me the extra ones from Augusta."

"Is there someone in Conyers that can go get them and meet me somewhere?"

"I don't know, but I'm going with Rain to her dorm room. Let me give you the directions."

"See if one of your dad's service people can bring the keys and I'll meet them on I-20. Call me back."

"OK. Thanks."

"How did you forget your keys anyway?"

"Girlfriend drama."

"Oh, well. You can tell me later."

"I see you're starting to smile," Rain teased after I hung up.

"You caught me. I'm smiling because I have a really great boyfriend. Even though he was a little upset, he can't stay mad at me. I'm really thankful I found him."

"Yeah, I feel you."

"The focus in a relationship should be on God. I finally realized that I was the one stunting my own happiness by not realizing what I actually needed in a man."

"Do you think you and Tad will get married?"

"Being that we're just freshman, I don't know. I know that I love him. Everything about Tad emulates Christ. That's the kind of guy I need. I can't imagine being with anyone else."

We waited an hour before Jordan came and picked us up. He didn't help us put our bags in the trunk. He just sat in the car.

Rain kept trying to strike up a conversation with Jordan, but he gave short answers. I could tell Rain was disappointed.

When he dropped us off I quickly said, "Hey, my boyfriend is coming down to bring my key at about twelve or so. Are you free to go to lunch?"

148

"Yeah, that's cool, just holler at me later," he said as he pulled off without saying anything to Rain.

"What did I do to him?" Rain asked. "I was just gone for a few days and now he's cold."

"Don't read too much into it."

"C'mon, Payton, you saw him. Something's up."

"Don't stress about it. We'll get to the bottom of it at lunch."

"That's easy for you to say. Your guy sounded happy to speak to you."

"Maybe there's something else going on. We'll just have to wait and see."

"I'm so glad you're here," she said as she hugged me.

"Let's get out of the rain, Rain," I said, teasing her.

The two of us walked arm in arm into her dorm room. Though we hadn't spent much time together, our friendship was still intact. We were there for each other. Whatever was going on with her and Jordan, I wanted to help solve the problem. I wasn't going to leave Atlanta until Rain had a clear understanding of where things were with the two of them. Even if that was an understanding that they weren't going to be an item.

Spelman College had a sophisticated security system. Rain had gotten Tad clearance and he still had trouble getting through. It was about 12:30 when he finally made it to take us to lunch.

Just as we were about to take off, Rain said, "Wait. I think I better call Jordan to let him know that we're leaving now. He's so impatient he might have left the restaurant."

I was glad she went upstairs because it gave me a chance to talk to Tad alone.

"So did you have a good trip?" he asked.

149

"There was a lot of tension. That's why I came back early. It's good to see you," I said as I gave him a big hug. "Look, there is something serious going on with this guy we're going to lunch with."

"Why are you telling me this? I don't know. Your friends change men faster than I change shirts."

"What's that supposed to mean?" I asked, noticing my guy getting a little salty. "I'm telling you so that maybe you can find out what's going on."

"I'm not prying into that man's situation."

"Well, that's my girl and I don't want to see her get hurt. All I'm asking you to do is talk to him. Maybe he will tell you something that he doesn't want to tell her. You could pass it on to me and I could tell her. Life would be great."

"That just sounds like a bunch of girl mess—something I am not at all interested in."

"Tad, please. She's hurting."

"If he offers the information, I'll tell you."

"Thank you, Tad."

Rain got back into the car and said, "He's still at the restaurant. It's a buffet near Clark's campus."

Jordan was waiting for us at the hostess area. He was a little nicer to Rain this time. He was real cool with Tad. They clicked.

"What's going on here in Atlanta?" Tad asked, trying to get everyone into the conversation.

"Things are crazy down here."

"Why did you choose Morehouse?" I asked.

"Why did y'all choose Georgia?" he asked.

"We both got scholarships," I told him. "Tad got a football scholarship and I'm on an academic one. Plus, I wanted to experience the real world before I got to the real world."

"I came to Morehouse because my dad went here. It works for me. We have a lot of pride at our school."

"It doesn't matter where we go to school," Tad put in,

150

"as long as we're puttin' somethin' positive in our heads. I'd much rather see a brother in school than in jail."

"Right, right," Jordan agreed.

After lunch, we followed Rain and Jordan to the airport. This gave me a chance to talk to Tad about Jordan.

"So what's up?" I said as we followed them. "What's wrong with Jordan?"

"He doesn't know if he's ready to commit. He likes Rain and all, but he wants to shop around a little more. He doesn't want to break her heart, so he doesn't want to get too deep yet."

"Oh, please," I said angrily.

"Why are you getting mad? I told you what you wanted to know."

"You make it sound like being committed is a bad thing."

"Payton, I love you, and this isn't about us. Not everyone is where we are yet. It's better that he let her know now than for them to get serious and he lets her go when he finds someone new."

"I guess you're right." I sighed, losing some of my frustration. "Am I supposed to tell her?"

"No. This is between Jordan and Rain. Don't say anything."

When we got to the airport, Rain said, "I know you know something, Payton. Spit it out."

I held her hands and said, "Talk to Jordan. Remember he's a cool guy. If you guys are supposed to be together then it will work out. Just remember to keep God first."

"He's gonna break up with me, huh?"

"Did I say that?"

"No, but why would I need God?"

"Tad and I are together and we still need God. Talk to Jordan and then call me."

Rain's eyes started to water.

Jordan, who was looking directly at us, said, "What's wrong?"

151

"You're gonna break up with me."

Tad got out of the car and said to me, "Why did you have to have a big mouth? Here's your key. I'll see you back in Athens."

I was in disbelief that this was happening. Tad got into his car and left. My heart was breaking for Rain and myself.

As I drove back to Athens in the rain I thought about my actions in the airport parking lot. I had to figure out what I could do to fix this.

"Why do I always have to be the one to fix things, Lord?" I sighed with frustration that had resurfaced.

When I arrived back in Athens I headed straight to my dorm room. I could barely get up the courage to talk to Tad. However, I dialed up his number anyway. Dakari answered.

"How have you been?" I asked, making conversation.

"Did you call to talk to me 'cause your boy ain't here?"

"What do you mean he's not there? I just saw his car."

"What? Are you stalking him or something?"

"No, I just drove by. Do you know where he is?"

"He went to the library with some girl. Did you hear me? She's so dope. I'd like to get with her. They are supposed to be studying, but I doubt that they are."

I tried to stay calm. "Thanks for the info."

When I hung up the phone I got in my car and went straight to the library.

After about fifteen minutes of searching for my guy I ran into Laurel. She seemed in deep thought, with her head against the bathroom door. She looked as if she had been fighting.

"Laurel," I said as a black girl brushed past me without even saying excuse me.

She looked startled. "Payton, what are you doing here?"

"Have you seen—"

"Tad?" she asked, taking the word from my mouth.

"Yeah."

"He was with some girl. I've never seen her before, but she and I just had a not-so-friendly conversation in the bathroom. She wants to get with him in the worst way."

"Look, I appreciate you sticking your neck out for me, but you didn't have to fight her."

"I know, but she really ticked me off. Something came out of me that I didn't know I had."

"What are you talking about?"

"You'd better go find him. I'll be OK."

I went around the corner and I couldn't believe the view before my eyes. The same chick who brushed past me in the bathroom was laughing and rubbing her hand on my boyfriend's face.

I walked up to Tad and said, "Can we talk, please?"

The mystery chick said, "We're studying. Please respect the fact that we have a test tomorrow and this is not social time."

"I wasn't talking to you," I said in the nicest way I could.

Tad got up and walked to the other side of the library. I could tell he had an attitude with me because I had found him up there, but I didn't care. This was our relationship and not some game.

"What, Payton?" he said.

"It's clear that this girl likes you, Tad."

"So? We're just studying. Why do you always have to be so jealous? I want a girl who can trust me. I want someone I can trust and when I say don't say nothin' she won't open her big mouth. You thought it was more important to tell Rain than to save her feelings, and right now I think it is more important that I study. We'll talk later. I'm not in the mood right now."

He walked away. I gained my composure and got ready

to leave. This was a trust issue and I wondered if we would survive it. At that uncomfortable moment, I was realizing the dilemma.

13

Bumping into Blessings

"Ouch!" I said as I misjudged the door on the way out and hit my head against the steel.

How could this be happening? Things were going so well between Tad and me, and now this.

I must have hit my head harder than I thought; it hurt a lot. I didn't have any aspirin at the dorm so I stopped at Eckerd's drugstore. When I got inside, my eyes were swollen from crying. I loved Tad and didn't want anything to mess up our relationship.

"Payton? Is that you, girl?"

I knew the voice, but I didn't want to turn around and have Robyn see me all distressed.

"Hey, girl," I responded without energy.

"I'm just getting back from seeing my friends. How was your trip? What's wrong?"

I couldn't answer her. Her concern made me cry even more. It was all so overwhelming.

We went and sat in her car and I told her everything.

"Why is my life going crazy? I thought I had a handle on things."

"Girl, fix what you can and let all the rest go."

"I wish it was that simple."

"Payton, people will let you down. When you give your problems to the Lord, you're supposed to let Him fix them."

"You're right, Robyn. I'm glad I ran into you tonight."

Robyn and I went into our dorm where I put on a gospel CD and let the music feed my soul. I wasn't going to try and fix it. I was just going to leave it alone.

I had left my textbook in the car and went back so I could get it. When I got to my car, there was a fine gentleman leaning against the driver's side door.

"Hey, pretty lady."

"What are you doing here?" I asked Tad.

"I wanted to apologize to you," he said as he started singing to me. "Please forgive me, Payton."

"What brought all this on?"

"Can we walk? I want to explain it to you."

As we walked to the courtyard and sat on the bench, Tad said, "Today, I guess I just got carried away. I should have been more sensitive to the fact that you were trying to protect Rain. When that girl came and asked if I wanted to study, I didn't see any harm in it. You were right. She wasn't really into studying at all. I owe you an apology."

"What made you come around?" I asked.

"She tried to kiss me. I told her I had a girlfriend and I left. I came straight here. I have been waiting for a little while."

"You were so angry, I didn't get to tell you that I didn't tell Rain. I only hinted, which was bad enough. I owe you an apology too. I just wanted her to be prepared."

"We can't always fix things, baby. Sometimes you just have to pray for folks."

"I still haven't talked to her. I don't even know what happened between them."

After we forgave each other we sat on the bench and looked up at the stars while thinking about the only link keeping us together, Jesus Christ.

Robyn and Tad were both right. I couldn't fix everything, but I was happy I knew a Savior who could. I still had a lot of other issues that were unresolved, like Cammie, cheerleading, Dakari, and my girlfriends. But sometimes we spend so much time worrying about what we don't have that we forget what God has blessed us with. I was in the arms of my man and that was only because of the grace of God.

It felt as if both of us were wrapped in the arms of the Lord. It was a beautiful feeling and one I would never forget.

School was back in and it was a little too soon for me. Tad was escorting me to my class when we bumped into his friend Casey.

"I haven't seen you in a while, man. Where have you been?" Tad asked.

"Just studying."

"I've probably been to the library one time in the whole year and you're there every night."

"I like studying there. It gets me away from all you crazy football players," he joked.

"Hey, Casey," I said.

"Hey, Payton. How are you doing?"

"Good. How about you?"

"I'm good."

"I still want to introduce you to my roommate."

"No, no, no, Payton. I'm fine."

"Casey, c'mon. It will be fun."

"I'll talk to Tad about it later. I'll see you guys," he said as he walked off.

"All right, man. I'll have to see what's in that library."

"Just books, Tad. Just books."

"Why did you say that?" I asked Tad.

"I saw him in the library the other day and he had a huge smile on his face. I think he knows some girl there."

"I think he and Laurel would be good together."

"Payton, don't try to fix the world's problems."

"Just see what you can do, Tad."

"You haven't even gotten Laurel to agree to go."

"Don't worry about that. It's already done."

Later that afternoon I was at cheerleader tryouts and talking to Laurel in the locker room.

"No, Payton. I am not going on a blind date. Do I look that desperate?"

I knew Casey was right for her and they would make a cute couple.

"It's hot in here," Laurel said. "I need to buy some water." She went through her purse for some change but came up empty handed.

I handed her some coins.

"Thanks, Payton. I'll pay you back tomorrow."

"You can keep it if you go on this blind date for an hour. If you don't like him then I'll never bother you about him again."

"Fine, Payton."

The first day of tryouts went very well. The cheers came easily for me, but Laurel seemed to be having some trouble. When we got home, we went over the cheer almost a hundred times until she got it. Later, I went to get a bite to eat while Laurel went to the library.

When I got back home, I knocked on the bathroom door and opened it at the same time. I saw Jewels, said,

"Excuse me," and went back into my room.

I did a double-take as I realized she was reading the number-one bestseller of all time—the Bible.

"Payton, come back. I need to ask you a question."

"No, I'll wait until you're done."

"I wasn't using the bathroom. I just needed some quiet time to myself."

"What are you reading?"

"Nothing really. I'm just skipping through. I'm confused as to where to start. I was wondering if you had any suggestions."

I sat on the end of the tub and we started reading at the beginning of the book of John, which is all about who God is and who Jesus is. Jewels was full of questions and I was thankful the Lord equipped me with answers.

It had been a long time since I had studied John, but I guess there are some things you don't forget. Like my favorite verses in the whole book, John 20:30–31: "And many other signs truly did Jesus in the presence of his disciples, which are not written in this book: but these are written, that ye might believe that Jesus is the Christ, the Son of God; and that believing ye might have life through his name."

I told her that Jesus was the bread of life and John tells it all.

Jewels started crying because she wanted God to be her Lord and Savior. She was tired of being bitter and into herself. She wanted to know she belonged to the King.

"I want to know Him," she said. "Nothing is going right."

"Give it all to Him, Jewels. He'll save you. There is more to this life than living and dying."

I prayed the prayer of salvation with her and it was like witnessing a miracle. This was the first time I had led someone to Christ. Jewels kept hugging me. It was as if she was a totally different person.

"I'm so glad I know you, Payton."

"Girl, you better be glad you know Jesus, because He's got your back."

Our talk was interrupted when the door to our room was slammed shut. I quickly went to see what was going on. It was Laurel and she was very emotional.

"Girl, what's up with you?"

"I'm ready to go on that blind date. When can you set it up? If he can go out then so can I."

"What are you talking about?"

Laurel flew past me and went into the bathroom to start taking a shower. I wanted to talk to her, but she didn't want to open up.

The week flew by. Laurel and I were holding hands while we waited to hear our names called on making the first cut for cheerleading. They were going in alphabetical order and we took a deep breath when they got to the Rs.

"Shadrach, Laurel. Simmons, Leslie. Skky, Payton . . ."

We jumped up and down with excitement.

"What are we going to do to celebrate?" Laurel asked.

"Tonight is the blind date, and Tad and his friend are going to take us out."

As we watched the girl who didn't make the cut leave, we realized how blessed we were.

On our way to meet Tad at Pizza Hut, Laurel told me why she was so jittery about meeting someone new. She said that a lot of her time at the library was because she had met a new friend. She liked him, and when she found out he was going on a date she was crushed.

"Just give my guy a chance, Laurel. I think you'll like him."

When we got to Pizza Hut, Laurel stood behind me as we walked over to Tad and Casey, who were already sitting down.

Tad gave me a big hug.

"Hey, Casey," I said as I stepped aside and presented Laurel. "I want you to meet my roommate, Laurel Shadrach."

They both turned red.

"It's you." Casey finally spoke.

"It's you," Laurel replied back.

"Man, what's going on?" Tad asked.

"This is the girl from the library."

Casey kissed her on the cheek and they sat down. It was the funniest thing. Laurel and Casey were a great match after all.

It was early May and all was well in my life. Tad and I were blissfully happy. Laurel had a smile plastered on her face that no one could take away. And the Lord had used me to lead someone to Christ. There were still some things I hadn't resolved, but that was OK. I was truly thankful for all the blessings I had received.

Karlton, the editor of the school newspaper, asked me to write a column. At first it was supposed to be a column for women, then African-American women, and then he changed it to freshmen. I was OK with that because I was trying to move on past racial issues. I had something in common with everyone at this school. We were all Georgia Bulldogs.

What could I say in the article? I wrote a testimony about my freshman year. When I came to Georgia, I had a different attitude from the one I would be leaving with after my first year. Initially I didn't have Georgia Bulldog pride, but now I knew what that pride was all about. I did a lot of growing up as a freshman, but the one thing I learned was that I loved my school and, if I had the right attitude, my school would love me back.

In my article, I stole a few words from a former president of the United States. I wrote:

"Ask not what UGA can do for you, my fellow freshmen, but before you come back to Athens in the fall, ask what you can do for UGA. If that's your mission, our university will be even better, even stronger, and an even greater place for all of us to be. Go, Dogs!"

Because Karlton put my picture beside the column, I got stopped by tons of people congratulating me for writing such a great article.

After talking to a few people, I said to Tad, "I know you're getting sick of all these people stopping us."

"Baby, I'm excited that they're proud of you. It makes me feel special. It was a great article."

I grabbed his arm and slid my body next to his. He was so sweet.

Another person stopped me. But he didn't like the article and had the nerve to say it to my face.

"I wrote the article because that's how I feel," I said to my classmate. "It does not have to be the way you feel."

"I don't want you to paint it like it's all great. Just because I'm a white male at UGA, everything is supposed to work out for me. I didn't get into the fraternity I wanted. My freshman year is not going good at all. So you know what UGA can do for me? I want them to give me my money back. But it's not that simple. I thought your article was stupid."

"Stupid might be a little harsh, but I understand what it's like to want something and not get it. I also understand being mad. I don't know if you believe in God, but that's why I was able to write that article. God loves me and He will take care of everything."

"I'm a Christian, too, but I guess I never looked at it that way."

We talked for fifteen minutes. Although he was white, we found we had much more in common because we both lived to serve God. When the guy was gone, I had given him a little hope. I looked around for Tad but couldn't find him. I heard him around the corner, and he sounded a little defensive.

"I don't know why you think there is anything between us," he was saying. "We only went to the library together. I have a girlfriend and I'm very happy."

When I rounded the corner, I froze. That girl from the library was trying to push up on Tad.

Tad said something as I slowly walked up to him. I was happy that he was my guy. The girl huffed and walked away. As soon as Tad turned around he bumped into me.

I hugged him. "Thank you."

"I love you," he told me.

"I know," I said. "I'm so glad I have you. Finding you was like bumping into blessings."

14

Fixing the Strife

I'm really worried about Dakari," Tad said to me as we
drove through the line at a fast-food restaurant.

"Why are you so worried?"

"He hasn't been home in two nights. Coach called to ask
if I had seen him."

"You can't worry about him. You've been telling me to
give stuff to the Lord. You've got to do the same."

"I've been praying, but something is wrong."

The serious look on Tad's face and the severity of his
words sent shock waves through my body. A vision flashed
before me of the evening news headlining the story of
Dakari's body being pulled from a lake. I don't know why
I thought it, but Tad was right. Dakari had not been himself.

"He's fine," I told Tad, hoping my words would come to
pass.

It had been raining for a while. It was as if the storm had
decided to pack up and take up residence in Athens. The

roads were extremely wet and I hoped wherever Dakari was he was being cautious.

Tad's cell phone rang and he answered it. "What? Man, slow down, I can't hear you. Hold on. Where are you?"

"Tad, what's going on?"

"It's Dakari. He didn't sound too good. We've got to go get him."

We got out of the line.

"Talk to me," I said.

"He was riding on 138 and he got into a wreck. I don't know much else."

Tad placed his hand in mine and we prayed as he drove. "Father, we ask that You be with Dakari. He needs You."

A little while later we came to an empty road. I saw Dakari's red Ferrari flipped on its side and all smashed up.

"Oh my gosh!" I said.

Dakari was on his knees in the rain without an umbrella, praying to God.

Tad and I jumped from the car and ran to Dakari's side. I had never seen him in this much despair. Something serious was going on. He stood up when we got to him.

I held the umbrella over the three of us.

"God saved my life. I am now bowing to the Father up above," Dakari said.

The umbrella almost slipped from my hand.

"What happened?" Tad asked.

"I was driving fast, ready to end it all because life is so hard. The next thing I knew the car lost control and started flipping. I started praying. Now I'm safe without a scratch. God is all I needed and He saved me. I miss my brother, but with one more roll, I would have hit that tree and been with him. I want the kind of joy that you two have. I know that type of joy comes from Somebody who is watching over us. I don't know what to do next. Tad, thank you for praying for me, man."

Lightning struck, and my hair was dripping, but I didn't care. A great miracle was happening right before my eyes. Dakari Graham was finally ready to accept the Lord. I felt like dancing in the street.

"If the lightning strikes me now, I know it's not the end for me."

"That's right, man," Tad told him. "Because one day Jesus is coming back for all of us. I can't wait to teach you everything I know about Him. The only thing that's gonna matter in the end is if you know God."

The two of them hugged.

As we all got into Tad's car, Dakari's car rolled over and hit a tree. Now it was totally damaged, but that was OK. God got Dakari out of the car. For the first time ever, Tad, Dakari, and I were of like mind. It was all about the King of kings, the Lord of lords. Dakari, Tad, and I were all excited about God.

"Payton, thank goodness you're here," Laurel said to me in a state of panic.

"Oh, no. What now?" I asked.

"Both Jewels and Robyn are walking around like depressed zombies. I heard they just got their results from dance team tryouts."

What could I say to them? Why would they talk to me when they wouldn't talk to Laurel?

I peeked into their room and Laurel was right. It was like stepping into despair. They looked so sad.

"What's wrong, you guys? Obviously you didn't make the team," I said when neither of them spoke.

Jewels got up to leave. "I don't know why Robyn is so sad. She made the team and I didn't."

"Robyn, what's wrong?"

"I don't think I deserve to be on the dance team. I'm the only black girl who made it. I kind of think maybe Jewels should have had the last slot."

"Why?"

"I still think I should be punished and shouldn't get any privileges. I had an abortion in high school. I don't deserve any good things. I should have been cut. That would have been my punishment for killing my baby."

"First of all, you are already getting your punishment by beating yourself up. Maybe you need to talk to your mom. Have you read any of her books?"

"No. I just can't believe I murdered my baby."

We sat there and cried. I was all out of words for her, but I felt her pain. Shayna told me once about a Christian group that dealt with postabortion issues. I mentioned it to Robyn so that maybe she could go and heal.

"You've got to let it go, Robyn. God has forgiven you, and unless you forgive yourself you will never get the chance to truly be happy. You need to go out and celebrate. Today's a good day. God made it and He made you."

Laurel knocked on the door. "Telephone, Payton. It's Dakari."

"I'm going to talk to Jewels, Robyn. Can you talk to him for a minute?"

"Sure."

As I went to find Jewels I prayed, "Lord, thank You. I don't know if I helped Robyn, but I definitely felt you talking through me. I need you to help me again."

I found Jewels in the lobby with puffy eyes.

"So you didn't make the team, huh?"

"It's not fair. I always make everything. I don't understand. I didn't have God all those times, and I made everything, and now that I have Him I didn't make it. Why didn't I make it? I was better off without Him."

"That's not true. I'm trying out for cheerleader, but if I

don't make it that's OK because I know God has something bigger and better planned for me. I've been where you are, but believe me, you are better with Him than without Him. He has something good for you, and you've got to be ready for it."

She hugged me tightly and smiled. I felt joyful inside. I was truly becoming my brother's keeper. I was caring for others' pain and helping them get out of it. That was my new purpose.

Jewels and I prayed, and after that I knew God was going to send her a miracle. God is good, and not just sometimes, but all the time.

I was in the room practicing my splits when the phone rang. I was surprised to hear Rain, Lynzi, and Dymond's voices.

"You know I was wrong, right?" Dymond said. "I was trippin' because I was jealous of you."

"Yeah, me too," Lynzi said. "I was jealous of all you guys. After this enlistment I'm quitting the army and getting back into school. That's where I need to be. I was wrong. After y'all left I got into it with Dymond."

Dymond announced, "Oh, yeah, Payton, I found your keys. I put them inside your gift and they should get there tomorrow. Since I can't keep a secret, I might as well tell you what I got you. An imitation Coach bag."

"Girl, why?"

"'Cause while you were up here I took forty dollars from your purse."

"I forgive you, girl," I told her.

Rain said that after the airport incident she gave Jordan some space and he came back to her.

"We've got to be there for one another always," Lynzi said. "I've got friends in the army, but none like you guys."

"I know that's right," Dymond put in.

"What are you thinking, Payton?" Rain asked.

I realized God had given me some good friends in college, but none of them could compare to my girls from high school.

Before we hung up we prayed like old times. Maybe our friendship had gotten out of whack because we hadn't put God first. But I truly loved Rain, Lynzi, and Dymond, and I thanked the Lord that they loved me.

As soon as I hung up, I did a split that was straight and effortless. It was a sign. When you give God the hard stuff, it's not all that hard anymore.

Laurel walked in and said, "Wow! What a great split!"

"I'm a little nervous about tryouts," I told Tad on the phone.

"It's OK. I'll pick you up and we'll go get some ice cream. Dakari and I were gonna study the Word some, but he said he had a hot date. I'll tell you about it when I get there."

As I threw on some jeans and a T-shirt, I thought about Dakari going on a date. I had to admit it bothered me a little.

As I got into Tad's car he said, "Why do you look so sad? Is it because Dakari is out on a date? Do you want him back or something?"

"I'm not even gonna answer that."

Neither of us said anything as we sat there eating our ice cream.

"There's your boy," Tad said sarcastically. "Now you can tell him you want him back."

I turned around and saw Dakari with Robyn. I couldn't believe it.

"Hey, girl," she said as she tried to hug me.

"Hey, Payton," Dakari said.

I rolled my eyes at them and stormed off.

"When did all this start?" I asked Robyn as she followed me to Tad's car.

"A few days ago when you asked me to talk to him on the phone. We met that night and we both prayed and cried. It was wonderful."

"I don't want to hear it. You didn't ask if you could go out with him. You know he's my ex-boyfriend."

"That's the key word. *Ex*-boyfriend. You're supposed to be in love with Tad."

"I am, but you're not supposed to be with Dakari just because I'm not with him." I walked back to Tad and said, "Are you ready to go?"

Dakari looked confused, Tad looked angry, and Robyn looked sad. Three people were going through it because of me. At that moment I didn't care. I was full of attitude that was in no way fixing the strife.

15

Feeling Totally Happy

"I got this, man," I heard Dakari say to Tad as I stormed off to the car once again.

"C'mon, girl," Dakari said. "I don't know what's going on, but I know you love Tad. What's up? I finally started goin' out and you get a little rattled."

"Don't flatter yourself," I told him.

"It's obvious you've got issues with me being with Robyn. What's the problem? I know you still have a little feeling for me, just as I have for you. The way I look at it, we wanted two different things. You wanted to be about God's business and I wanted to get busy. Now my perception has changed, but you need to be with Tad. Robyn's your girl and I found out that we are in the same place in our Christian walk. You and Tad are at the same place too. God has given me a new friend in Robyn."

"It's not that I want you, Dakari. It's just that I don't want anyone else to have you. That's pretty shallow, right?"

"Just a little. Don't you want me to be happy? If being

with different people is going to make us better people, then we've got to support each other with our choices."

"How do I make this right?" I asked.

"I think you know."

I gave him a big hug and thanked him. The two of us walked back to Tad and Robyn.

I kissed Tad on the cheek and said, "I love you. Forgive me."

When I didn't say anything to Robyn immediately, I guess she thought I was still mad at her and she excused herself to go to the bathroom.

"I'll be right back," I said to Tad.

Tad held onto the tip of my finger and I could tell he was still disappointed.

"Do you forgive me?" I asked.

"Yeah. But I want you to be real with what you're feeling. I don't want you to be with me out of obligation or anything."

"Tad, you know I love you. It wasn't that I wanted Dakari, I just didn't want him to be with anyone else. I'm with who I want to be with. And more importantly, who I am supposed to be with."

He smiled at me as his cell phone rang. "Go check on your girl," he said.

The bathroom wasn't big enough for two people so I waited for Robyn to come out. Her eyes were puffy.

"Can I talk to you for a second?" I asked.

"Payton, I didn't try to backstab you," she said softly. "I apologize for not being sensitive to your feelings. Dakari and I are just starting, but I can stop it before it goes any further. You already have a place in my heart, and I don't want to lose that."

I took her hand and said, "I was a jerk. Dakari needs somebody like you. He needs someone who loves the Lord, and you do."

"Are you sure yo're cool with me talking to him?"

"Yeah. Maybe the two of you can find peace like Tad and I have. Go for it."

She gave me a big hug, and we walked back to Tad and Dakari. I really had grown in the year, and things were good.

"I just got a call from Coach Mullens," Tad said. "He and his wife are barbecuing and they suggested that we come over. Y'all down?"

"For a picnic?" Robyn said. "You know I am."

"Oh, yeah," I said. "I wanna stop at Wal-Mart and get a gift for the twins."

It was cool. Dakari and Robyn followed Tad and me to Wal-Mart and then to the Mullenses' house. That afternoon was full of fun, food, and true spiritual blessings. Shayna talked to Robyn and me inside while Coach Mullens talked to Dakari and Tad outside. One of the babies started crying and Robyn went to see what was wrong.

"So, Payton," Shayna said, "I see you're with Tad, but you're also here with Dakari and his new friend. How do you really feel?"

"Shayna, I'm there for Dakari, and I want him to be happy. I'm sure he and Robyn will have drama, but I'll stay out of all that. The Lord will take care of them."

"Wow, Payton! You're growing in the Word and that brings total happiness. When you know God you can weather the changes and be better for it."

Tad looked at me through the window and blew me a kiss.

"He really cares for you," Shayna said.

"I know. I feel the same. I just don't want it to go wrong."

"Don't focus on that. Keep doing what you're doing. Keep being honest and keep praying together daily. Enjoy where you are. Don't rush life. I'm proud of you, and I know God is too."

173

"So am I," I told her.

"Wow," Shayna said. "What a reason to feel good."

"Our seven female cheerleaders' names are going to be announced in alphabetical order," the coach announced. "When I call you, come out to the center of the court. Congratulations to Becky Adams, Tristan Collins, Kayla Denny, Leslie Simmons, Laurel Shadrach, and Carly Weindberger."

Dejection set all over my face.

I heard Willie behind me say, "You didn't make it. You should have gone home before you embarrassed yourself."

God, You are good. I thank You for allowing me to try out, I thought, not allowing tears to fall.

Then the coach said, "Wait, I forgot one. That was only six. Let me look at the list again. Let's see. We have Becky Adams, Tristan Collins, Kayla Denny, Laurel Shadrach, Payton Skky, Leslie Simmons, and Carly Weindberger."

"Oh my gosh!" Laurel screamed.

I didn't hear the announcement because I was still thanking the Lord in the midst of being disappointed.

The girl next to me nudged me and said, "They called your name."

I got up and walked in amazement to the center of the court and hugged Laurel with a feeling of complete joy. After announcing the girls, the coach announced the guys. Ironically, Willie, who had made fun of me, didn't make the squad.

There were so many people congratulating me I almost got tired of hugging, but when I saw Tad's proud face, chills ran up my spine. He picked me up and spun me around and kissed me in the midst of everyone. It felt great.

After he put me down he said, "Someone else wants to congratulate you. It's your other favorite guy."

"Where is Dakari? What silly thing does he have to say?" I asked.

"I thought I was your favorite guy," my dad said, coming from nowhere.

"Daddy!"

My mom stood beside him and said, "Payton, I'm so proud of you."

"How did you guys know?"

"Tad phoned us and told us to come support you either way," my dad said. "We know it wasn't easy for you to make it."

"Where's Perry?" I asked. "Now that he's got his license he thinks he's too grown up to come and see his sister, huh?"

"I'm here," Perry said. "You've always been there for me and now I'm here for you."

My brother was growing up fast. He was getting a mustache and everything. I couldn't wait to hug him.

"Mr. Skky, I just want to say congrats to your daughter, sir," Dakari said, trying to get past my dad.

"Boy, what's been up with you?" he asked Dakari.

"I'm just tryin' to get it together."

"I understand."

"Mom, this is Robyn," I said. "She has Dakari's eye."

"Oh, really?" my mom said. "You girls need to watch out for each other. Where is Laurel? Her family is here."

When I found Laurel we hugged each other and cried. This was what it was all about. I had lifted God in uncertainty and given Him complete reign over my life and He had blessed me.

The celebration was so long, Laurel and I never got a chance to talk. We went to a buffet dinner together with our families, our boyfriends, and our suite mates. Even Jewels came along.

Before I could head into my dorm room I heard a voice say, "Payton, can I talk to you for a second?"

It was Cammie.

175

"I heard you made cheerleader," she said.

"Yeah, thanks," I said, keeping my distance.

"I just wanted to tell you that because of what you said to me, I went back to my room, read Scripture, and prayed that the Lord would help me get my life together. I've been going out with this really cool guy in my science class. I think he likes me, and I like him. He's white, so don't be shocked."

"Girl, I don't care," I said, giving her a hug without even thinking. "As long as you're with a great guy, I'm happy for you."

"Thanks, Payton. I feel better about myself than I have ever felt. God made me, and if I'm fine to Him then I'm all right to me."

"Payton, come here!" I heard Laurel yell.

"Girl, I'll talk to you later," I said as I gave Cammie one last hug.

When I walked into my room, I was amazed to see dozens of red and white roses. Georgia colors.

A note said, "Congratulations, ladies. We will play harder next year because we know you will be there to cheer us on at every game, home or away. We're so proud. Tad and Casey."

We heard a knock on our window and saw Tad and Casey smiling and holding up a congratulations sign.

Just when I thought the night couldn't get any better, girls from our dorm came to cheer and clap for us. A place that had held misery now held bonding.

I was thankful that God had allowed me to do all the things I had.

At the end of the night, Laurel and I gave roses to everyone who had come to visit, and we still had tons left.

I got on my knees and prayed. "Thank You. Thank You for sending Your Son to die for me. Thank You for allowing me to tell others about You. I love You. Amen."

Finals were coming and I had to study at the library. Things were changing at Georgia. Karlton Kincaid won SGA president. He asked me to be the director of minority recruitment, and I accepted.

I was learning what my life was about. It wasn't about me but about God. I didn't know what was next for me, but I knew the Lord was in my life.

I couldn't study when I got to the library so I pulled out my Bible. I read Psalm 13. I got a revelation. God was here. He had always been with me and He would never leave. I shouldn't be anxious about anything. I was trusting more and more that He would work things out.

After being spiritually fed and studying for an hour, I realized I needed some food in my stomach. I packed up my stuff and left. I ran into a girl who looked familiar.

"Hey, your name is Payton, right?"

"Yeah, where do I know you from?"

"I work in the cafeteria."

It hit me. She was the girl I thought was a student first semester, but it turned out she had a baby and was taking care of her.

"What are you doing here?" I asked.

"Last semester, when I talked to you, you inspired me to reach beyond my circumstances and let the Lord show me a better way. You told me that I could do more than I was doing. I was able to get a grant and now I'm here. I'm studying for finals."

"Girl, that's great! Here, take down my number and we can get together. What's your name again?"

"Drea," she said. "I'm so glad God used you to help me."

"Lord," I said as I walked to my car, "I didn't realize I was witnessing when I was talking to her. Thank You for using me."

"Grandma, how are you really doing?" I said to my dad's mom as we sipped her famous *tecolade*—her concoction of tea, Coke, and lemonade.

"I'm fine. It's just tough around this time of year with it being near Mother's Day and my birthday. Your grandfather always did something special for me this time of year. He would always wash my feet."

My papa was gone but not forgotten. He was a man who loved the Lord above everything else. He knew no harm would come his way because God was in control.

On Mother's Day weekend my family drove to Conyers to spend the day with my grandmother. Tad, Laurel, Casey, and I were going to Six Flags.

Before I could finish my last sip of tecolade, I saw my beau driving around the corner.

"Payton, I tell you, you've got a good one," my grand-mother said, not letting Tad leave. "I want to tell you two that dating is never easy. You're brother and sister in Christ first. Y'all are gonna be fine. I have a feeling you will be together for a while. Y'all go on to Flags Six and have a good time."

"Six Flags, Grandma." I laughed as I gave her a kiss on the cheek, and she hugged me tightly.

About two hours later, the four of us were having a great time riding all the roller coasters.

"Payton, I'm glad the Lord allowed me to room with you this year. You've been like a sister."

I also wanted to talk to Laurel, but I didn't know how she would take my news. Robyn and I wanted to room together next year because we were so close.

Out of the blue Laurel said, "Maybe next year we don't have to room together." She explained that she was going to try living in the sorority house for a year. When I told her about my plans, she laughed.

"I love you, girl," I told her.

"I love you, too, Payton. Thanks for pushing me and Casey together. We probably would have just kept meeting in the library without telling one another how we felt. I like him a lot. He is everything I liked in my high school boyfriends, Branson and Foster, plus so much more."

The guys came bearing cotton candy and snow cones. Night was starting to fall and that set the mood. I was at a good place in my life. I was confident in who I was and had a pretty good vision of where I was going.

Tad and I sat on a bench while Laurel and Casey went for a walk.

"You're beautiful, Payton. I see Christ in you. You have taught me a lot."

"Can I have a hot dog?" I said as we sat there pigging out on Six Flags gourmet.

We were crazy about each other, but we were even more crazy about God. In addition to that, my parents were doing well, my brother was doing great, my friends were on top, and my grades were good. At that moment I was feeling better than I thought I could because I had given it all to Him. Over the last two years, I had learned that if I sought Him first, everything else would fall into place. At that moment, when Tad kissed me, he left some mustard and ketchup on my cheek. That made us both crack up. At that moment, things couldn't be better. We were feeling totally happy.

ISBN: 0-8024-4236-6

Staying Pure

Payton Skky has everything a high school senior would want—popularity, well-to-do parents, and excellent grades. To top that off, she dates the most sought after boy in her school, Dakari Graham. However, when Dakari puts on the pressure to take their relationship to the next level, Payton goes numb. Torn between what her soul believes and what her heart wants, she struggles to make the best decision. Will her choice be the right one?

Sober Faith

Payton Skky just had the night of her life—introduced to society as a debutante with a bright future, and things were back on track with her new boyfriend and escort, Tad Taylor. However, when it comes time to celebrate, Payton's friends want to toast with something other than punch. Though she wants to be down with her girls, Tad warns her that the consequences could be severe. Which will win...the flesh or the Spirit?

ISBN: 0-8024-4237-4

Saved Race

Payton Skky is about to accomplish a life-long dream—graduate from high school with honors. However, when Payton's gorgeous, biracial, cousin, Pillar Skky steps on the scene and Payton has to deal with feelings of jealousy and anger towards her. Though she knows God wants her to have a tight relationship with her cousin, years of family drama seem to keep them forever apart. Will Payton accept past hurts or embrace God's grace?

ISBN: 0-8024-4238-2

Sweetest Gift

Payton Skky now has what she's always longed for—to go to college and live away from home. Though she quickly finds out that being an adult is not easy. When Payton feels her new friends have it goin'on, she begins to lose self-confidence and starts to feel she doesn't fit in. She can't seem to let go of her sad feelings. Can her relationship with Jesus Christ fill her with joy she lacks?

ISBN: 0-8024-4239-0

MOODY
PUBLISHERS

THE NAME YOU CAN TRUST.

1-800-678-6928 www.MoodyPublishers.com

SURRENDERED HEART TEAM

ACQUIRING EDITOR:
Cynthia Ballenger

COPY EDITOR:
Chandra Sparks Taylor

COVER DESIGN:
Lydell Jackson

INTERIOR DESIGN:
Ragont Design

PRINTING AND BINDING:
Versa Press Incorporated

The typeface for the text of this book is
Berkeley